"Who are you?"

"What?" Trish answered, frightened by O'Neill's sudden question.

A cold wind ruffled the linen tablecloth, and the chill cut through her layers of clothing and made her shiver. She was intensely aware of the vulnerability of her situation, alone in the wilderness with a man she barely knew. Did O'Neill know more about what had happened to her sister than he'd let on? Even more frightening was the possibility that he might have been responsible in some way for her sister's disappearance.

Trish pushed away her fears. Tales of evil spirits, ghosts and strange lights had affected her reason. O'Neill had been the epitome of kindness and consideration since their first meeting. She had no reason to fear him.

She hoped.

Dear Harlequin Intrigue Reader,

It might be warm outside, but our June lineup will thrill and chill you!

* This month, we have a couple of great miniseries. *Man of Her Dreams* is the spine-tingling conclusion to Debra Webb's trilogy THE ENFORCERS. And there are just two installments left in B.J. Daniels's McCALLS' MONTANA series—*High-Caliber Cowboy* is out now, and *Shotgun Surrender* will be available next month.

* We also have two fantastic special promotions. First is our Gothic ECLIPSE title, *Mystique,* by Charlotte Douglas. And Dani Sinclair brings you *D.B. Hayes, Detective,* the second installment in our LIPSTICK LTD. promotion featuring sexy sleuths.

* Last, but definitely not least, is Jessica Andersen's *The Sheriff's Daughter.* Sparks fly between a medical investigator and a vet in this exciting medical thriller.

* Also, keep your eyes peeled for Joanna Wayne's THE GENTLEMAN'S CLUB, available from Signature Spotlight.

This month, and every month, we promise to deliver six of the best romantic suspense titles around. Don't miss a single one!

Sincerely,

Denise O'Sullivan
Senior Editor
Harlequin Intrigue

MYSTIQUE
CHARLOTTE DOUGLAS

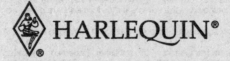

HARLEQUIN®

TORONTO • NEW YORK • LONDON
AMSTERDAM • PARIS • SYDNEY • HAMBURG
STOCKHOLM • ATHENS • TOKYO • MILAN • MADRID
PRAGUE • WARSAW • BUDAPEST • AUCKLAND

ISBN 0-373-88626-8

MYSTIQUE

This edition published by arrangement with Harlequin Books S.A.

® and TM are trademarks of the publisher. Trademarks indicated with ® are registered in the United States Patent and Trademark Office, the Canadian Trade Marks Office and in other countries.

www.eHarlequin.com

Printed in U.S.A.

ABOUT THE AUTHOR

The major passions of Charlotte Douglas's life are her husband—her high school sweetheart to whom she's been married for over three decades—and writing compelling stories. A national bestselling author, she enjoys filling her books with love of home and family, special places and happy endings. With their two cairn terriers, she and her husband live most of the year on Florida's central west coast, but spend the warmer months at their North Carolina mountaintop retreat.

No matter what time of year, readers can reach her at charlottedouglas1@juno.com, where she's always delighted to hear from them.

CAST OF CHARACTERS

O'Neill—Handsome and mysterious resident manager of Endless Sky resort.

Trish Devlin—She'd used all of her abilities to search the wilderness surrounding Endless Sky for her sister.

Quinn Stevens—Reclusive billionaire, owner of Endless Sky, he's been dubbed The Last Man Standing by Wall Street. His true identity is still a mystery.

Debra Devlin—Trish's sister, a reporter who goes to Endless Sky to interview Stevens…and then disappears.

Victoria Westbrook—Wealthy heiress in search of a husband. Is that the only reason she's come to the exclusive resort?

Chad Englewood—Real estate investor who claims he was cheated by Stevens. Is it his desire for revenge that caused Debra to go missing?

Captain Metcalf—Sheriff's deputy in charge of the search for Debra Devlin.

The Averys—An elderly couple from Atlanta.

Judd Raye—The resort's custodian.

Ludie May Shuler—A maid at Endless Sky. She has keys to every room….

Henri—Endless Sky's sous chef. He knows just what to put in the food. And what not to.

Janine Conover—Assistant resident manager.

Tiffany Slocum—Another reporter seeking an interview with Quinn Stevens. How far would she go to get it?

Michael Redlin—Nashville music producer.

Dan Beard—Owner of Kentucky racing stables.

Austin Werner—Independently wealthy from a secret source.

Chapter One

Trish Devlin stepped from the dimly lit, air-conditioned school corridor into the harsh afternoon light. In spite of the intense heat, she shivered with a sudden sense of foreboding, as if a shadow had blocked the sun, and her breath caught in her throat. She stopped short, ambushed by an unexpected wave of negative emotions, but the sensation of imminent disaster passed as quickly as it had arrived, leaving her wondering whether her sixth sense had activated or her imagination was playing tricks.

Humidity engulfed her like wet cotton batting and dispersed the remnants of her sudden chill. The blazing Florida sun had turned the school's parking lot into a hot, shimmering pond of sticky asphalt. She hurried to her car, closed tight against forecast thunderstorms, and opened the door to an interior hot enough to bake bread. With a sigh, she thought enviously of her sister Debra, financial reporter for the *Tribune,* on assignment in the North Carolina mountains, where early October meant refreshingly cool days and crisp, chilly nights, not the unending sizzling sauna of a Tampa summer.

But, Trish thought as she waited for her car's interior to drop a few degrees, she wouldn't trade jobs with Deb for anything, and certainly not for the sake of a better climate. Trish loved her work as a seventh-grade teacher and welcomed the challenge of shaping young minds. Her students, teetering on the brink of adolescence, vacillated erratically between childhood and maturity and filled her days with perpetual surprises. She had to scramble constantly to keep up with their brief attention spans. Reporting business news as her sister did, even if the career took Trish around the world, could never match the satisfaction of helping children learn.

Thinking of Deb, Trish smiled, until the eerie chill struck her again. She hoped she wasn't coming down with something. She didn't want to turn over her newly trained classes to a substitute teacher only eight weeks into the new school year.

She climbed into the car, slid gingerly onto the hot upholstery and started the engine. After she switched the air-conditioning to its highest setting, the car cooled quickly, creating a pleasant temperature for the long ride home along the Suncoast Parkway into the rural countryside of North Tampa. In spite of her physical comfort, however, Trish's emotional uneasiness grew, frayed her nerves and filled her with unnamed worries that made her skin feel too tight for her body.

I'm just tired. I need to put my feet up, have a glass of wine and de-stress after a day with one hundred and fifty overactive and sometimes pain-in-the-butt preteens.

Twenty minutes later, she turned onto the cul-de-sac in the suburban neighborhood where her home backed onto a preservation area of cypress woodlands. The sight of a plain black sedan parked in front of her house sent her anxiety level skyrocketing.

Debra?

Trish reached deep inside for the psychic connection she'd shared all her life with her younger sister, her only living relative. Instead of Debra's usual comforting presence, she found only emptiness.

She parked in her driveway and climbed out of her car. A man and woman, dressed in dark business suits, exited the sedan and approached her.

"Patricia Devlin?" the man asked.

Dry-mouthed, Trish nodded.

"I'm Agent Cox, FBI." The man flashed his ID and gold shield. "This is my partner, Agent Jernigan. May we speak with you?"

Trish unlocked her front door with fingers that had suddenly turned clumsy, led the agents inside to the sunny living room that overlooked the woodlands at the rear of the house and offered them seats. She sank onto a white rattan sofa across from the agents and clasped her shaky hands in her lap. Their expressions were grim. Their news couldn't be good.

"When did you last speak with your sister?" Agent Cox asked.

Oh, dear God. They really were there about Debra. "Yesterday morning."

"And you've heard nothing since?" The female agent's voice was brisk, all business, but her eyes were kind.

Trish shook her head. "But that's not unusual. What's this about?"

Agent Cox leaned forward, and Trish, focusing on insignificant details to keep from coming apart at the seams, noted the strands of gray in his closely trimmed dark hair, the tiny lines around his eyes and the heavy gold college ring on his right hand.

"Our Asheville office," he said, "contacted your sister's editor at the *Tribune* earlier this afternoon before calling us. Ms. Devlin has been missing for over twenty-four hours."

"Missing?" Trish shook her head in disbelief. "But she's staying at Endless Sky Resort on the Blue Ridge Parkway. Didn't anyone check there?"

"The resort's manager is the one who alerted the FBI to Ms. Devlin's disappearance," Agent Jernigan explained. "No one at Endless Sky has seen her since early yesterday, and this morning, one of the guests found her cell phone on a seldom-used hiking trail."

"Maybe she checked out," Trish said, grasping at straws. *Deb, where are you?*

A resonating psychic silence was her only reply.

"She didn't check out," Agent Cox said. "Her clothes and laptop are still in her room. And the resort is as remote as they come. Most guests arrive and depart by helicopter. The only access road is more like an all-terrain challenge course, passable only by four-wheel drive vehicles. Even the most seasoned trailblazers wouldn't simply hike out of Endless Sky. The nearest town is over thirty miles away."

Trish looked from one agent to the other. "So you think she's lost in the mountains?"

"Local search-and-rescue teams have been activated," the female agent said, "but it's a massive wilderness area."

Trish breathed deeply in hopes of easing the tightness in her chest, but worry for Debra formed a steel band around her lungs. She wished the agents would leave. She had to get to North Carolina to search for Deb herself. "Thank you for notifying me."

The agents exchanged glances. "We have a few questions," Agent Cox said.

Trish unclenched her fingers where her nails had dug crescents in the palms of her hands and tried again without success to relax. "What do you need to know?"

"What was your sister doing at Endless Sky?" Agent Jernigan asked.

Trish frowned. "Her editor didn't tell you?"

"Newspaper people play their cards close to their vests," Cox answered with a scowl, "to protect their sources. Her editor just said she was on assignment."

"A big assignment," Trish said. "She was hoping to interview Quinn Stevens."

"The Last Man Standing?" Agent Jernigan's eyes went wide with surprise before she recovered her composure. "Is he at Endless Sky?"

"He owns the place," Trish said, "and he's rumored to spend time there, disguised as one of the guests."

Quinn Stevens was an urban legend. While still in his teens, he'd developed an Internet company that made him an instant multimillionaire. His keen business sense had prompted him to sell just before the dot-coms went under in the nineties, and he'd invested his profits in real estate, which earned him billions. One of the few original entrepreneurs to survive the dot-com debacle, Stevens had been dubbed "The Last Man Standing" in a *Wall Street Journal* article. The nickname had stuck. Today, the reclusive entrepreneur—few, if any, knew what he looked like—had more money than Oprah. An interview, especially with accompanying pictures, would have been a major journalistic coup, one Debra had been determined to achieve.

"Did she get her interview?" Cox asked.

"She was hopeful," Trish said. "When I spoke with her last, she said she was close to figuring out who he was." The direction of their inquiries struck her. "You don't think Quinn Stevens has anything to do with Deb's disappearance?"

"In order to find your sister," Agent Jernigan said gently, "we have to be open to all possibilities."

"Which brings me to my next question," Agent Cox said. "Does your sister have enemies, anyone who might wish her harm?"

Trish shook her head and wished she could dispel the icy dread that consumed her. "Everyone loves Deb."

"Even the people she's written about?" Cox said.

"Deb's exposed some shady dealings in her articles over the years," Trish admitted. "The participants in those schemes weren't too happy to see their names and unsavory business practices in print."

"Any of them ever threaten her?" the female agent prodded.

Fear for her sister sent a shiver down Trish's spine. "Deb's had a few threatening phone calls and e-mails. Someone egged her car in the newspaper parking lot once. But her editor will know more of the specifics than I do. Deb always laughed off the threats around me."

As if responding to a silent signal, the agents stood at the same time and Cox offered his card. "If you hear from your sister or think of anything that might be helpful, let us know."

Trish took the card and walked them to the door. "Please, call me on my cell phone if you find out anything. Or leave a voice message on my home phone."

She rattled off her numbers, then closed the door behind them.

Deb was missing.

Her knees buckled and she leaned against the door. Panic threatened to consume her, and she fought against the engulfing hysteria. Ever since their parents had died when Trish was five and Deb was three, Trish had taken care of her younger sister. She wasn't about to abandon that lifetime habit now. Drawing a deep calming breath, she thrust her fears aside.

She hurried to the desk in the living room, extracted a pad of paper and a pencil from the drawer and turned on her computer. She and Deb were as different as night and day. Deb was the flighty one, the risk taker, the adventurer. Trish had always been the steady sister, the problem solver, the organizer. First, she called her principal and arranged for personal leave. Then she hurriedly made her list, checked Web sites and reached again for the telephone.

Her sixth sense, a special gift as strong as her telepathic link with her sister, insisted that Deb needed her help, and Trish had a plan.

LATE THE FOLLOWING morning, Trish gripped the arms of her tourist-class seat with white-knuckled fingers as the plane sank through heavy clouds for an instrument approach to the Asheville airport.

Forget Trish Devlin, she reminded herself for the umpteenth time. *From now on, you're Erin Fairchild, and you have to think of yourself as Erin or you'll give everything away.*

She mentally cataloged what she knew about her destination. After the FBI agents had left yesterday, she'd searched the Web for information on Stevens and his resort. She'd also recalled bits and pieces of her talks with Deb about Endless Sky.

"I could never afford this place if the *Tribune* wasn't picking up the tab," Deb had said during her first call home from the resort. "It's definitely where the rich and famous get away from it all."

"Sounds interesting."

"More than interesting." Deb's voice had crackled with excitement. "It's a puzzle. I get the distinct impression that nothing here is what is seems, including the guests. Some of them must be registered under fake identities for anonymity."

Trish was about to try her own hand at deception. If she went bumbling into Endless Sky with everyone aware that she was Deb's sister, she'd be treated differently than if she were just another guest. And if someone was hostile toward Debra, Trish would probably be the last to know. In disguise as Erin, she could snoop around all she needed to and also monitor results of the search for her sister.

I love you, Debster. You have to know how much, especially since your fear-of-heights-and-flying sister has boarded a plane and is now headed toward the highest point on the Blue Ridge Parkway to find you. I'm praying the cloud cover means I won't have to travel to the resort by helicopter.

The plane taxied to a halt. Trish gathered her carry-on bag and purse and hurried through the Jetway. The first object that caught her eye upon entering the concourse was a large white poster board with Erin Fairchild printed across it in bold black letters. She took a second to register that the sign was intended for her.

Next to attract her notice was the man holding the poster board. At over six feet tall and standing a head above the crowd of tourists and reuniting families, he would have captured her attention even without the conspicuous poster. The first word that came to mind was *mysterious*. Even in the midst of the milling throng, he exuded a sense of solitude and aloofness, as if surrounded by an invisible force field that caused the pulsing crowd to cut him a wide berth as they pressed past him toward the luggage carousels.

Her next impression was *interesting*. The majority of travelers were dressed in blue jeans, sweaters and other casual clothes, with only a few in business suits. Her greeter, however, was attired completely in black, with Italian boots of the finest leather, impeccably creased lightweight wool slacks and a finely knit black shirt, topped by a sleek leather jacket that accented the breadth of his shoulders, the nip of his waist and his narrow hips. Thick black hair brushed the collar of his shirt and the midnight-blue of his eyes was so dark that they might as well have been black, too.

"Ms. Fairchild?" His deep, husky baritone broke her reverie and made her aware that she'd been standing in front of him, staring.

"Yes. Erin Fairchild," she said to remind herself as much as to answer his query. She didn't have to worry about anyone noticing a resemblance to her sister. Deb looked like the pictures of their father, tall and athletic with dark hair and eyes. Trish, petite with blond hair and blue-green eyes, favored their mother.

"I'm O'Neill, manager of Endless Sky. I'll be driving you to the resort."

"Thanks for meeting me."

"All part of the service." His attitude was formal, but not cold. Not particularly friendly, either. "If you'll come this way, the car's out front." He folded the sign, tossed it into a nearby receptacle and reached for her carryall.

Car, not helicopter. Thank you, God. "My other luggage—"

"—will be delivered to the car by a skycap." He motioned for her to precede him across the terminal, and she headed toward the exit.

Ah, I keep forgetting that the rich are different. Rule Number One: never carry your own bags.

O'Neill, who had apparently exhausted all conversation, said nothing further as they crossed the terminal. But she could feel his scrutiny as he walked behind her, a tingling sensation between her shoulder blades, like an itch she couldn't scratch.

Outside the main building, O'Neill directed her toward a large SUV, an impressive custom sky-blue Hummer with the resort's logo, a silhouette of an Adirondack-style lodge perched atop a rock ledge and Endless Sky in rustic lettering, painted on the side.

He opened her door and held out his hand to give her a boost into the Hummer's high seat. Just before she gripped his hand, another presence brushed her mind.

She froze and stifled a gasp. *Deb? Are you there?*

She received no reply.

O'Neill's dark eyes narrowed. "You okay?"

"Muscle cramp," she improvised. "From sitting too long on the plane."

Even if she hadn't been traveling incognito, she wouldn't have tried to explain the psychic connection she had with her sister. Only the two of them shared that secret, a trait they had inherited from their mother. Trish's earlier memories of communicating with her mother and sister had been a silent understanding, without the need for spoken words. After they'd been orphaned, the girls had been sent to live with their elderly great-aunt, whose dominant rule of child rearing was that children should be neither seen nor heard. As a result of their aunt's strictness, the little girls, desperate to communicate, had developed their budding psychic ability into full-blown telepathy. When their aunt had isolated them in separate bedrooms, they learned to carry on telepathic conversations to console each other's loneliness. They'd maintained their ability into adulthood, although distance negated the kind of full-blown dialogues they'd managed when living together. They could communicate fully only if in physical proximity to each other.

Trish had always considered their telepathic abilities a blessing, a shared trait that strengthened the bond between her and Deb. She intended to use that skill and the heightened sixth sense it had given her to find her sister.

"You can let go of my hand now." O'Neill's deep voice, tinged with irony, broke through her thoughts.

She glanced from her hand, clasping his so tightly that his tanned skin whitened beneath her fingertips, to the hint of amusement dancing in his deep blue eyes and broke the contact instantly.

"Sorry," she murmured.

"You were a thousand miles away."

"Still at home." She forced a bright smile. "Wondering if I remembered to pack everything."

He angled his head to one side and considered her with a long, searching look that raised goose bumps on her skin and made her aware that there was more to O'Neill than met the eye. "And home is?" he asked.

"Palm Beach," she said quickly. "I stopped in Tampa on the way up to visit old friends. College roommates. I've known them forever. Couldn't pass through town without seeing them."

She shut up and mentally kicked herself. She'd been babbling. She shouldn't explain too much. She'd only raise suspicions.

"Palm Beach." His expression turned thoughtful. "So you're one of *those* Fairchilds."

"Distant cousin," she lied hastily, having no idea whom he was talking about. She studied his tanned face with its sharply chiseled cheekbones, broad forehead and generous mouth for signs of disbelief.

O'Neill didn't bat an eye. "It's a big family."

He closed the passenger door, saving her from further explanations, rounded the Hummer and opened the hatch for the approaching skycap to load her luggage into the rear of the SUV.

Her bags were almost new, purchased for a vacation in Aruba last summer, but they had obviously been bought at Sam's Club, not Saks. She hoped O'Neill wouldn't notice. Her wardrobe would be the diciest part of her deception. Her clothes were stylish and good quality, but definitely not designer or even top-of-the-line, except for a few outfits bought at a secondhand consignment shop. Maybe she could pass as a penny-pinching eccentric. At least she had Aunt Samantha's diamonds to wear to the resort's formal dinners to aid in her disguise as a wealthy guest. She swallowed a sigh. This little jaunt had cleaned out her savings account, but she'd gladly take out a second mortgage on her house if it meant finding her sister.

O'Neill tipped the skycap and climbed into the driver's seat with the easy grace of an athlete. The lowering clouds, which had held off until now, unleashed a steady rain.

O'Neill switched on the windshield wipers and drove out of the airport lot.

Lulled by the hypnotic swish of the wiper blades, Trish gazed out the window for a glimpse of the famous Blue Ridge Mountains. She saw only gray clouds and walls of dripping foliage.

"So," O'Neill said after they'd passed through the quaint downtown district of Hendersonville, "why are you here?"

"What?" Her heart pounded in her throat. Did he suspect already that she was an impostor?

"Some of our guests come for the solitude," he explained, his gaze on the road, his tone conversational. "Others for hiking and white-water rafting. Some are here just to see and be seen. What brings you to Endless Sky?"

Unaccustomed to deception, Trish felt her mind whirl like tires in mud. If she answered solitude, she'd have no excuse to mingle with the guests to discover all she could about Debra's interactions before she disappeared. If Trish opted for hiking and white-water rafting, she'd spend too much time away from the resort to find out anything helpful. And to admit she'd come to rub elbows with the rich and famous seemed gauche and obviously nouveau riche.

But wasn't that part of her disguise?

"I'm not much of an outdoors person," she said, stalling for time until she could come up with the right words to explain her trip. "But I *adore* meeting new people," she gushed and tried to keep from blushing at her over-the-top performance. "I'm also here to escape the heat. We won't have cooler weather in Florida until November."

"The weather's always cool at Endless Sky," O'Neill said. "Often wet and cool, like today. But on sunny days, you can see for miles from our porches. The resort is famous for its spectacular views."

They had left the town behind and were driving along a narrow, two-lane highway that wound through a thick forest, whose branches, heavy with rain, overhung the road and created the impression of a tunnel lined with dripping, deep green leaves, a few tinged with a hint of color. The Hummer's headlights glistened on the dark wet pavement ahead.

In the enclosed confines of the vehicle with soft rock playing on the expensive sound system, she found herself intensely aware of O'Neill. The heat funneling through the vents carried the aroma of his fine leather jacket, a balsam-scented soap and a pleasantly masculine aura. His long, tanned fingers gripped the steering wheel with practiced ease. He wore no wedding ring, an ambiguous deficiency. Under other circumstances, she would have found the man, with his arresting profile and mysterious air, attractive, but she'd come to North Carolina to find her sister, not a significant other.

A significant other.

For a while, she'd hoped that Brad Larson, the physical education coach at her school, might fit that bill. As much as she loved teaching, she'd give her career up in a heartbeat for the right husband and children of her own to love and nurture. All her life, she'd wanted a family, and Brad had seemed to share her goal. But as good a friend as he'd been, he didn't make her heart sing or her pulse pound. She feared, however, that the kind of love she longed for was a myth, the stuff of romantic movies and bestselling novels. At twenty-nine, if she wanted children, she couldn't wait forever for a knight in shining armor to steal her heart. Maybe she'd give in this year to Brad's proposal.

But first, she had to find Debra and she might as well pump O'Neill for information while she had him as a captive audience. "Is the resort full?"

He nodded. "You were lucky to get a room at such short notice. We had one guest, uh, cancel unexpectedly. The fall leaf season is our busiest time of year."

A canceled guest. Did that mean Trish had been placed in Debra's room? Had they given up hope of finding her sister? And what had been done with Deb's belongings? She peered through the passenger window at the unrelenting greenery and breathed deeply to steady her voice. "When do the leaves begin to change?"

"They've already started at the resort's altitude. If you stay for the two weeks you've reserved, you'll probably see the colors peak."

If she stayed? Why would he say that?

"I like meeting new people, but I'm not fond of large crowds," she said, turning to a safer subject. "How many guests are there?"

"Although Endless Sky is huge, we have only eight suites. Smaller numbers create a more intimate experience for our guests. We rarely have over sixteen registered at a time, fewer when most of the suites are single-occupancy, as they are this season." He cast her an appraising glance. "Some of our guests have met the man or woman of their dreams at Endless Sky."

She suppressed a shiver. Had Debra met someone who'd ultimately been responsible for her disappearance? "I'm not in the market for a husband," she assured O'Neill, but with just enough of a laugh and lilt to her voice to deny her assertion. The Erin Fairchild she'd conceived as her cover would be ditzy enough to be in the market for almost anything.

He smiled, as if at a secret joke. "Then some of our other female guests will be less inclined to scratch your pretty eyes out. I know one or two who are here specifically to snag a wealthy husband. You'd put a real crimp in their style."

Was O'Neill flirting with her? While his words had been complimentary, his demeanor remained aloof. The contradiction increased his air of mystery. Maybe flattering female guests was part of his job description. Unable to think of an appropriate response to his comments, she remained silent.

O'Neill turned off the highway onto a road even more narrow and winding than the last. "We're on the Blue Ridge Parkway now," he announced. "It takes us along the tops of the mountain ridges. If the weather weren't so cloudy, you'd find the views breathtaking."

The Hummer's engine strained on the steep grade that led them higher into the mountains and the clouds. At times, visibility was almost zero, but O'Neill seemed undisturbed by the enveloping mists and drove with the confidence of a man who knew exactly where he was going. At one point, the clouds parted to reveal a sheer drop of thousands of feet just beyond the shoulder of the road, and her fear of heights kicked in. The view was breathtaking, all right. In seconds, she'd be hyperventilating. Assaulted by her phobia, she could barely draw air, and beads of perspiration gathered on her forehead. She closed her eyes against the dizzying vista and forced several deep breaths to stave off panic.

O'Neill, apparently oblivious to her distress, guided the Hummer along the torturous curves, and they met no oncoming traffic. Everyone else, she thought with irony, had better sense than to drive in such weather, especially on such a precarious route.

When O'Neill turned off the highway

onto what looked more like a dry creek bed than a road, a check of her watch indicated they'd left the airport an hour ago.

"This is where the Hummer makes all the difference," the resort manager commented.

She opened her mouth to reply, but a jolt from traversing the roadbed filled with huge rocks caused her jaw to snap shut and she bit her tongue.

"Can't the resort afford a proper road?" she asked, mainly to see if her tongue still functioned.

O'Neill threw her a smile. "What? And spoil the mystique? One of the draws of this place is its inaccessibility. If just anyone could drive up to the front door, it wouldn't be exclusive, would it?"

Trish gripped the edge of her seat as the SUV lurched up the steep incline through the overhanging evergreens. She felt as if she had entered another dimension, a world of shadows and mystery where the unknown lurked just beyond her sight. She wondered how O'Neill could see the road. Every tree, shrub and boulder was shrouded with gray mist and slick with moisture. Wisps of clouds formed and dissipated, like ghosts that materialized, then disappeared.

The tough suspension of the Hummer couldn't absorb every jarring bounce in the rugged road and by the time they reached the top of the ridge, she was wishing the weather had been clear enough for the helicopter. At least arriving by air, although equally terrifying, would have been over faster.

O'Neill, however, didn't seem to mind the bone-rattling passage. He navigated the rocky trail with an irritating calm.

But thoughts of O'Neill vanished as the huge bulk of Endless Sky loomed through the clouds. The massive three-story resort perched on the jutting ledge of mountain among granite outcrops like a giant predatory bird. Shrouded in fog and mystery, with its numerous gables, encircling porches and towering balsam firs, the resort appeared more like the set for a Stephen King movie than a luxury hotel and brought to mind tales of Tar Heel ghosts and Cherokee legends she'd read as a child.

She shivered from the pervasive dampness and an unnamed fear. Isolated from the world by distance and an almost impassable road, she was entirely on her own.

Deb?

Her mind reached out to her sister, but a deathly silence was still the only response.

Chapter Two

O'Neill crested the top of the ridge and guided the Hummer onto the gravel drive that circled the wide, formerly well-tended lawn at the rear of the resort. Intended for the guests' enjoyment of croquet, volleyball and picnics, as well as used as a helipad, the area was now a sea of churned grass and mud, the recent staging area for four-wheel drive and all-terrain vehicles used in the search for Debra Devlin. He made a mental note to call the landscapers to repair the damage as soon as the search had ended.

The ATVs and pickup trucks of the search-and-rescue teams had departed temporarily earlier this morning. While waiting for the weather to break, the volunteers would grab some sleep, hot food and dry clothes and be ready to hit the trails again when the cloud cover lifted.

Clear skies were forecast for the evening, and the sheriff's department's helicopter, equipped with infrared heat sensors, would sweep the mountainsides again, looking for signs of a warm body.

Warm being the operative word.

If Debra Devlin had fallen to her death from one of the paths that skirted cliffs and ravines, the chopper wouldn't spot her. But if she were alive and merely lost, the equipment would be invaluable in locating her among thousands of acres of wilderness and rough terrain.

The woman's disappearance had been a nightmare. For over an hour last night, the FBI had grilled O'Neill in his quarters, a two-story cottage separate from the resort. He'd cooperated as best he could, not only for the sake of the resort but because he liked Debra Devlin. Her exuberant, unassuming personality had been a breath of fresh air among the self-absorbed guests who now filled the lodge. O'Neill hoped she'd be found soon and unharmed.

"We know Ms. Devlin was here to interview Quinn Stevens," the senior agent had told him. "Is Stevens among the guests?"

O'Neill shook his head. "I can assure you that Mr. Stevens isn't a guest, nor has he been a guest this season."

The agent studied him with a dubious glance. "You're sure? I understood that no one knows what this Stevens guy looks like."

"Stevens is my boss," O'Neill said. "I'm the only one at Endless Sky who's ever met him in person."

"Can you describe him?"

"About my height and weight. Midthirties. Brown hair, brown eyes. Ordinary," O'Neill added. "He wouldn't stand out in a crowd."

"We'll need an address where we can contact him."

O'Neill had reluctantly complied and given them the address and phone number of Stevens's home in Monterey, California.

Stevens hated intrusions on his privacy, but a disappearance at the resort he owned demanded desperate measures.

"Were any of the guests offended by the fact that Ms. Devlin was a reporter?" the younger agent asked.

"Offended so much that they might have caused her harm?" O'Neill shrugged. "You'll have to ask them. Most, like me, were probably unaware of her profession until after her disappearance."

He'd unlocked Ms. Devlin's suite earlier that day to allow the agents access. Once they had bagged, tagged and removed any belongings and all evidence pertinent to their search, O'Neill had directed Judd Raye, the resort's custodian and handyman, to secure the remainder of the reporter's effects in a locked storage closet in O'Neill's cottage. After an okay from the feds, O'Neill had sent the housekeeping staff to prepare the suite for Erin Fairchild's arrival. Even if Ms. Devlin was found, her room had been reserved only through yesterday.

He cut a glance at the attractive blonde in the passenger seat. She'd called for a reservation late yesterday afternoon, hours before news of Debra Devlin's disappearance had hit the media. Otherwise, he'd have suspected that Erin was a journalist, anxious for firsthand coverage of the search.

Reporters, he thought with a grimace of distaste. Even Endless Sky's remote location wasn't protection against their annoying intrusion. Once the weather cleared, they'd descend like vultures in their news helicopters with camera lights blazing and microphones bristling like spines on a porcupine's back, insensitive voyeurs to a terrible tragedy and a colossal pain in the ass to his wealthy guests.

He drove the Hummer under the porte cochere on the resort's north side and killed the engine.

"Welcome to Endless Sky, Ms. Fairchild."

"More like endless clouds," she grumbled and stretched in her seat, as if to ease aching muscles.

O'Neill held back a smile. Erin Fairchild was no rich playgirl. He'd recognized that fact the moment he'd first seen her. Not that she wasn't knockout pretty with eyes the color of tropical seas that made a man want to take a plunge. But she lacked the skillfully molded, carefully coiffed, tortuously manicured and obviously expensive clothing of the wealthy females who usually frequented Endless Sky. He'd bet a year's income that her pale, shoulder-length hair was natural blond, her flawless peaches-and-cream complexion had never undergone a surgeon's scalpel or BOTOX injections, and her trim physique, deliciously rounded in all the right places, was not the result of the rigorous regimen of a personal trainer.

No, there was nothing fake about Erin Fairchild's appearance, but O'Neill couldn't shake the distinct impression that she was hiding something. Her clothes and luggage didn't fit her wealthy persona. Either she was an eccentric who didn't spend much money—then why was she here?—

or a working girl who'd splurged to mingle with the rich and famous for a couple of weeks. Or maybe she was another reporter determined to make a name for herself by capturing an interview with the elusive Last Man Standing. If so, that interview was never going to happen. Too bad for her, O'Neill thought, because he liked what he'd seen so far of Erin Fairchild.

The grizzled face of Judd Raye, the resort's rangy caretaker, appeared at the passenger door, and he opened it for their new guest. With a wince of discomfort, Erin slid from the SUV and glanced around, a futile effort in the enveloping mist.

O'Neill climbed from the driver's seat and rounded the vehicle to her side. "Not much to see in this weather, so I'll give you an inside tour."

While Judd gathered Erin's luggage, O'Neill escorted her into the huge lobby. He was pleased to note that the housekeeping staff, despite their time-consuming interviews with law enforcement, had not neglected their duties. A cheerful fire popped and crackled in the massive fire-place whose stones rose the height of the two-story ceiling. A trio of enormous ant-ler chandeliers cast a glow from the high vaulted beams onto the mission-style fur-niture grouped in conversational clusters below. Decorative displays of Cherokee ar-tifacts and mountain handicrafts had been straightened and dusted. Several of the guests relaxed in the comfortable chairs, reading, chatting or simply staring into the fire. Gigantic arrangements of colorful dahlias, chrysanthemums and native joe-pye weed centered the coffee tables and decorated the fireplace mantel and main desk. The flowers' fragrance mingled with the woodsy aroma from the fireplace. All was in order.

Erin had stopped inside the double doors and was gazing around the room as if searching for someone.

"Would you like to meet a few of the guests now?" O'Neill asked.

She blinked, as if coming out of a trance, and shook her head. "I'll wait until dinner."

O'Neill gestured toward the main desk. "If you'll sign the register, I'll show you to your suite."

The smile she gave him almost took his breath away. It lit her face, like the sun dispersing the clouds. "You're very kind."

He shook his head. "All part of my job, Ms. Fairchild."

At the desk, she took the pen and registration card he handed her. She faltered slightly after she began to write, scratched through what she'd completed, then tore the card in half and slid the pieces in her pocket. "The rough ride left me a little shaky," she said with an apologetic grin. "I'll need another card, please."

"No problem." O'Neill removed a blank registration form from a cubbyhole behind the desk and gave it to her. This time, she completed it quickly in a bold, firm handwriting.

"Did you have lunch on the plane?" he asked.

"No." That electric smile hit him again. "But I'm not really hungry."

Never let it be said, O'Neill thought, that any guest at Endless Sky went without a meal. At the per diem rates they were paying, they could eat all day if the urge struck them. "I can have the kitchen prepare something light and deliver it to your suite."

"On one condition." A hint of flirtation laced her dazzling smile.

O'Neill was accustomed to being hit on by female guests. And even a few of the guys. It went with the territory. In the past, without exception and without interest, he'd politely diverted all overtures. His miserable experience with Alicia had inoculated him for life against wealthy, calculating women. But Erin Fairchild was different. He found himself wanting to know her better, to discover exactly who she was and why she was here. He couldn't explain why he felt drawn to the woman, but he was certain his attraction was caused by more than the hint of sadness and desperation he glimpsed beneath the surface of her carefree attitude.

He wondered if Erin had come to End-less Sky to escape some tragedy. An un-happy relationship? A broken heart? A failed career? What event in this attractive woman's life had caused her to flee to the wilderness and immerse herself in the company of affluent strangers? O'Neill considered it his personal quest to find out.

"What's your condition for letting me order you a meal?"

"You've missed lunch, too. Will you join me?"

Overriding his usual inclination to remain aloof, he returned her smile. "If you like."

He called the kitchen and placed an order for two, then grabbed the key cards for the Mountain Laurel Suite from the rack behind the desk and motioned her to accompany him.

"Elevator or stairs?" he asked.

"Stairs, please. I want to stretch my legs after sitting so long in the car."

They climbed the broad stairway to the third floor and traveled to the end of the hall. Her scent teased him, cutting through the evergreen aroma used by the cleaning staff. He attempted to put a name to it. Obsession? Joy? One of the many Chanels? But her fragrance was more simple and natural than expensive perfume. With a start, he recognized the fresh, clean smell of Irish Spring bath soap, perfect for a woman named Erin. He smiled at the simplicity, unlocked the suite and opened the door to the sitting room with a flourish.

"Your home away from home, Ms. Fairchild."

"Please, call me Erin." This time, the trace of sadness was even more evident beneath her engaging smile. She preceded him inside.

O'Neill executed a quick visual reconnaissance of the room. All traces of Debra Devlin were gone.

Judd had placed Erin's bags on racks at the end of the oversize canopied bed in the adjoining bedroom, visible through open double doors, but Erin ignored them. She walked through the sitting room and ran her hands over the furniture like a blind person fingering Braille, as if trying to read some message from their surfaces.

"Is the room to your liking?" O'Neill asked.

She looked around as if seeing it for the first time. "It's lovely."

He crossed to the French doors that led to a private balcony and opened them. "Take a look."

She stepped onto the dripping veranda but kept well away from the railing. "Nice view, if you like gray."

"Wait until tomorrow morning. When the sun rises and the clouds lift, you can see all the way to South Carolina and Georgia from this very spot."

Her cheeks paled and she stepped quickly back into the room. "I'll take your word for it."

Interesting. Erin was apparently afraid of heights. If so, why had she picked the highest point on the Blue Ridge Parkway for a vacation?

Before he could ponder that puzzle further, a rap on the door announced the arrival of room service. O'Neill opened the door and Ludie May Schuler, who'd been with the staff since the resort's opening and was dressed in its traditional forest-green uniform with a burgundy apron, wheeled in a loaded cart. With the efficiency of a well-oiled machine, she cleared the arrangement of fresh fall flowers from the sitting room's polished oak table, covered it with an immaculate burgundy linen cloth, and set it with fine bone china that sported the resort's logo and heavy sterling silver engraved with ESR.

"What have you brought us, Ludie May?" he asked.

The older woman lifted silver domes from two platters. "Egg salad, tuna salad, smoked salmon and cucumber finger sandwiches, fresh fruits, and petits fours."

In her drawl, she'd turned *petits* into *pity* and *four* into a three-syllable word, but O'Neill didn't mind. He'd learned long ago that his guests enjoyed the local mountain dialect. "Perfect."

While Ludie transferred the platters and

a silver tea service to the table, O'Neill touched a match to logs in the fireplace, then pulled out a chair for Erin.

Ludie May left and closed the door behind her. With obvious fatigue, Erin sank into the chair he offered and placed the burgundy napkin on her lap with shaky fingers. She appeared in need of a soothing vacation, he noted, and hoped that Endless Sky would fit the bill.

"You'll find it peaceful here." He passed the plate of tiny sandwiches and she took one at random. "And the mountain air will give you an appetite."

Her expression was dubious, and she left the sandwich untouched on her plate. "It *is* quiet. Do you ever have any excitement here?"

O'Neill sighed. The news would ruin their lunch, but he might as well tell her. She'd hear it from the other guests soon enough, and he couldn't hide the fleet of rescue vehicles that would converge on the resort once the weather cleared.

"Unfortunately, yes. Too much excitement. One of our guests disappeared the day before yesterday."

"Disappeared?" The color drained from her face but her seawater eyes sparked with intensity.

"We're afraid she became disoriented on one of the trails and wandered into the wilderness."

"Isn't anyone looking for her?" Her long, elegant fingers shredded her sandwich into crumbs.

"Search-and-rescue teams have been combing the mountains. But they've taken a break during the bad weather."

Erin's gaze strayed to the open balcony doors. "There're hundreds of square miles of forest out there. How will they ever locate her?"

"The teams know these mountains. And they're using specially trained dogs and helicopters with heat sensors. If she's out there, we'll find her."

"*If* she's out there?" Erin's pretty forehead wrinkled in a frown. "Where else would she be?"

O'Neill swallowed a sandwich and bit back the word *dead*. He regretted starting out Erin's vacation on such a somber note. He forced a smile. "Maybe she met the man of her dreams and eloped."

Erin's expression brightened. "Was she involved with one of the guests?"

He shook his head. "She was a very outgoing person who mingled with everyone, but no one in particular that I could tell."

Erin leaned forward, her lunch forgotten. "But Endless Sky is a big place. Even the most astute manager wouldn't know what goes on in every suite?"

"True," he admitted, "but none of the other guests is missing and the FBI has interviewed them all. No one could shed any light on her whereabouts."

"What's her name?"

"Debra Devlin." No reason to hold back. Erin would hear it on the news. "She's from Tampa. You said you have friends there. Ever heard of her?"

"No," she said quickly. "Tampa's a huge

city. Has anyone else checked out since this Debra disappeared?"

O'Neill shook his head. "Most of our guests come for extended stays. The ones who are here now will remain through the peak of leaf season."

Those amazing eyes that reminded him of sunlight dancing on a Caribbean lagoon skewered him with a piercing gaze. "Have the authorities ruled out foul play?"

He ate another sandwich while he carefully composed his reply. "They're pretty certain she's merely lost. Her cell phone was found on an isolated trail. She must have dropped it while hiking."

He wiped his mouth with his napkin and stood. His lunch with Erin hadn't gone as he'd hoped. Debra Devlin's disappearance had cast a pall that he couldn't shake. As attractive as Erin was, O'Neill's thoughts were filled with worry over the woman who'd disappeared. An approaching cold front would clear the clouds and once it arrived, at this altitude, the night temperatures would drop into the thirties. For a woman already weakened by exposure, thirst and hunger, hypothermia could be fatal.

"I should get back to work." He strode to the door, then turned toward Erin. "Would you like me to send Ludie May to help you unpack?"

"No, thanks. I can manage."

"Anything else you need?"

Erin looked suddenly vulnerable, and the desire to protect her surged through him. "I'm fine," she said, but she didn't sound fine.

"Then I'll see you at dinner tonight. It's one of our formal bashes, so you'll want to dress accordingly."

"Thank you, Mr. O'Neill."

"Just O'Neill is fine." He slipped through the door and closed it behind him.

While the elevator descended to the first floor, Erin Fairchild, an intriguing puzzle he was looking forward to solving, occupied his thoughts. He couldn't explain the sudden air of protectiveness he felt toward this most recent arrival, who was clearly a woman who could take care of herself. She hadn't broadcast an aura of helplessness, like so many of his female guests who were on the prowl for a man. She seemed centered, self-assured.

So where had his sudden urge to shelter her from unpleasantness come from?

Chapter Three

As soon as the door to the suite closed behind O'Neill, Trish released a deep breath, dug the torn registration card from her pocket and tossed the pieces into the fire. While the paper on which she'd printed her real name by mistake was devoured by flames, she allowed herself to relax for the first time since arriving at Endless Sky. Pretending to be someone else was exhausting, and she prayed she could maintain her disguise long enough to find Deb. At least in the privacy of her rooms, she could let down her guard.

She rose, crossed to the double balcony doors O'Neill had left open and closed and locked them against the encroaching cool, damp air. In spite of the logs blazing in the fireplace, she felt chilled to the bone. To disperse the shadows that reached out from every corner, she strode through the suite's sitting area, bedroom and bath, and turned on all the lamps and overhead lights. Even with the room ablaze with illumination, she couldn't shake the feeling that she wasn't alone. Preposterous as it seemed, she felt someone was watching, following her every move. Maybe tomorrow the sun would shine, she prayed, not only to aid in the search for Deb but also to banish the gloomy, depressing, almost creepy atmosphere of Endless Sky. Despite its lavish and tasteful furnishings, the lodge, a warren of claustrophobic hallways with innumerable nooks and crannies, gave her the willies.

Trish returned to the sitting room, poured a cup of lukewarm tea and gave herself a pep talk. She was imagining things. Her concern for her sister had her hypersensitive and sensing danger at every turn. Even the delectably handsome but mysterious O'Neill seemed somehow threatening, scrutinizing her as if he could read her mind and expose her charade. She knew too little about him to trust him and wondered why he used simply O'Neill as his name and if he had another to go with it. He certainly wasn't the Tom, Dick or Harry type, but a commanding man who'd have a forceful, unforgettable moniker, something dashing like Remington, Hunter or Blade.

In spite of her uneasiness in his company, she wished he had stayed longer. He'd been talking about Deb and she'd wanted to hear more, anything that might help her figure out what had happened to her sister.

Outside, the wind freshened and howled as if fighting to come inside. It buffeted the building until the massive structure shuddered, then screeched around its corners with a banshee cry. The double doors blew open, draperies billowed and thick gray mist poured into the room like an uninvited guest. The powerful gust of wind snuffed out the fire and swirled ashes over the hearth. At the same instant, every light flickered, dimmed and went out, plunging the suite into murky shadows.

Trish felt something brush against her elbow. She slammed down her teacup and rushed to close the doors once more. Their sudden opening rattled her because she was certain she had firmly secured the latch just moments ago. And she couldn't deny the sensation that someone—or something—had entered the room.

Deb? Are you here?

Her only answer was another shriek of wind that shook the windows and doors as if unseen hands were trying to get in. Trish breathed deeply to stave off the beginnings of a panic attack. She wasn't usually afraid of either the dark or being alone, but the eerie conditions at Endless Sky had her already-frayed nerves unraveling at a dizzying pace.

Concern for her sister brought a sob to her throat and tears to her eyes. If Deb was lost on the mountain in this weather, she was cold and miserable and would probably give anything to be back in the relative warmth and security of these dark and gloomy rooms that Trish found so depressing and intimidating.

A knock at the sitting room door startled her, and she felt her way through the shadows, bumping her knees and stubbing her toes against the furniture as she navigated a path to the door.

"Who's there?" she asked.

"Ludie May with housekeeping," a drawling female voice answered.

Happy for company, Trish unlocked and opened the door and almost screamed with alarm. The light of the fluorescent lantern the maid held at her waist threw distorting shadows upward across her face, creating a gnomelike effect. Trish bit back her startled cry and remembered how she and Deb as children had played in the dark with flashlights, holding them beneath their chins to create the same scary appearance.

Ludie May lifted the lantern and handed

it to her, and her weathered face resumed its former rough-hewn but nonthreatening aspect. "Thought you might want this. Storm's knocked the power out, but Judd'll have the generator going soon."

Trish accepted the lantern gratefully. "Thanks."

"And if you're through with lunch, I can clear them dishes for you."

"Please." Trish stepped aside to let the older woman enter.

Ludie May rolled in a cart from the hall and began loading it with dishes and the remains of lunch. "This your first time at Endless Sky?"

"Yes, it is." Trish placed the lantern on the mantel where it cast a feeble blue-white glow across the sitting room.

"Well, don't let folks scare you with talk of ghosts," Ludie May warned.

"Ghosts?" Although Trish had accepted her gift of telepathy years ago as a highly developed extension of what others called intuition, her belief in the paranormal didn't extend to roaming spirits of the dead. However, in the dark and gloomy atmosphere of the resort, almost anything seemed possible. "They're only stories, right?"

Ludie May glanced up from her work with a somber expression. "So some claim, but plenty folks have seen 'em."

"Have you?" Trish asked, humoring the woman.

Ludie May nodded solemnly. "This hotel was built on sacred Cherokee ground. Spirits still walk here."

Ignorant superstition, Trish thought, but kept the conversation going, hoping Ludie May would stay and keep her company longer. "But they're friendly spirits, aren't they?"

"Some are. Some ain't." Ludie May dropped her voice. "Just don't go off anywhere alone. I warned that Ms. Devlin, too, but she didn't pay me no mind."

"You think evil spirits are responsible for her disappearance?" Trish asked in disbelief.

"If'n they was good 'uns, would the poor woman be missing?" Ludie May insisted with contorted logic. She loaded the last dish onto her cart, pushed it toward the door, then paused on the threshold. "Ghosts appear even in daytime here, missy. You be careful."

With that cryptic warning, she rolled the cart away and shut the door behind her.

In that instant, either the custodian activated the generator or the resort's electrical connections were restored. Every light in the room blazed, causing Trish to squint in the sudden brightness.

Ghosts, she thought with a shake of her head. More likely, Deb had tripped and fallen somewhere, spraining an ankle so she couldn't return. When the search-and-rescue teams resumed operations, she assured herself, they'd discover Deb, bring her back to the resort, and the two sisters could enjoy the rest of their stay together while Deb's ankle healed.

A deep chill of foreboding destroyed whatever comfort Trish's self-assurances had given her and made her wonder if Ludie May had been right.

Were evil spirits stalking Endless Sky? And had Deb run afoul of them?

HOURS LATER, refreshed by a short nap, Trish entered the dining room that mirrored the architecture and mission-style furnishings of the lobby. Her earlier thoughts of evil spirits seemed silly among the lights, laughter and muted conversations of the gathered guests. Soft classical music wafted through the room, where most of the elegantly attired guests were already seated at several round tables covered with forest-green linen and set with Endless Sky's signature china and silverware. Heavy sterling, multi-branched candelabra surrounded by flowers and filled with lighted tapers centered each table and cast an intimate glow that complemented the blaze from the hearth.

"I've reserved you a chair, Erin." O'Neill appeared at her elbow, and she was happy to see his familiar face among the sea of strangers. "We rotate our seating every few days, so guests have an opportunity to get to know one another."

"That's great!" She flashed her best social-climbing smile and dug deep for the energy to project the right amount of ditzy enthusiasm. "As I said in the car, meeting new people is the main reason I'm here. I hope you've placed me with the best-looking single guys."

She suppressed a cringe at her blatant behavior and batted her eyelashes.

"You'll be at my table tonight," he said, his expression unreadable.

"Well, there you go." She threw him a glance that she hoped looked hot and flirtatious and not pathetically unpracticed. Too bad she couldn't have gone undercover as a wallflower librarian, a role for which she felt much better suited.

As he'd been earlier at the airport, O'Neill was dressed entirely in black. But tonight he wore a black tuxedo with a co-ordinating black collarless shirt, severe but fashionable, the style a Hollywood star might don for the Academy Awards. Its custom fit emphasized his handsome physique, and the severe black complemented his dark tan and the unusual deep blue of his eyes. She wouldn't have thought it possible, but he appeared even more handsome than he had this afternoon. And more dangerous. The kind of man who'd break a woman's heart without a qualm or backward look.

"I hope you weren't inconvenienced by the temporary blackout," he said.

Trish shook her head. "The resort seems to have prepared for every contingency."

"Not every," he murmured.

She followed his gaze to the glass doors that overlooked a broad terrace and the lawn beyond. Headlights and the beams of powerful handheld spotlights cut through the darkness and crisscrossed the lawn. The search-and-rescue teams had returned.

"The moon's almost full tonight," O'Neill said. "It will help the search."

Trish issued a silent prayer that they would find Deb and vowed to hit the trails for her own search at first light the next morning. Forcing another vampish grin, she slipped her hand through the crook of

O'Neill's elbow as he led her to the table nearest the fireplace.

At well over six feet, he towered above her, and she could feel the heat from the corded muscles of his arm through the expensive fabric of his tux. He threw her an engaging smile that exposed perfect white teeth, and she wondered if he ever grew tired of playing escort to the wealthy women who moved in and out of his life every few weeks.

Three other people were already seated at their table, and the two men stood as O'Neill pulled out Trish's chair.

The first was elderly, a rake-thin man, in his eighties at least, who accompanied a woman who was his contemporary. O'Neill made the introductions. "Mr. and Mrs. Avery, meet Erin Fairchild."

"Delighted, my dear," Avery said with old-fashioned gallantry and shook her hand before taking his seat.

Mrs. Avery, dressed in gray silk and multiple strands of pearls, inclined her head, a royal nod of both acknowledgment and dismissal.

"And this is Chad Englewood."

The second man, about O'Neill's age, blond, buff and attired in a traditional tuxedo, grasped Trish's hand and grinned widely. His breath held the aroma of too many before-dinner drinks. "Hel-lo, gorgeous. When did you get here?"

"This afternoon, just in time for the blackout." Trish settled in her chair between O'Neill and Chad.

Chad took his seat and leaned toward her. "Get used to it. One of the inconveniences of living in the wilds."

Considering the opulence of their surroundings, Trish couldn't help laughing. "If this is the wilds, I'd love to see civilization." She noted the empty chair on Chad's other side. "Will your wife be joining us?"

"God, I hope not!" he blurted, then laughed at Trish's shocked expression. "I have an ex-wife, who, please God, is still on the West Coast in Santa Barbara and will stay there."

"Victoria Westbrook will round out our table tonight," O'Neill announced.

"Where are you from?" Chad asked Erin, "and what brings you to Endless Sky?"

"I'm from Palm Beach, and I'm here to escape the Florida heat." She looked across the table to the Averys, intending to draw them into the conversation. Chad had latched on to her with an intensity she hoped to discourage, but the Averys' attention was riveted by a platter of hors d'oeuvres as they made their selections.

"Don't mind them," Chad said in a loud whisper. "They're not only deaf as posts, *she* won't have anything to do with the rest of us. Old money from Atlanta. She doesn't mix with riffraff."

Trish cut a glance at O'Neill, but his expression, as usual, was inscrutable. She had the distinct impression, however, that he was keenly aware not only of the conversation at their table but of everything else that was happening throughout the room as the uniformed waiters served the first course.

Hurried footsteps and the rustle of fabric announced the arrival of Victoria Westbrook. The striking redhead in her late twenties wore a strapless dress of copper silk that exposed creamy shoulders and showcased a necklace of diamonds, topaz and gold filigree. Her upswept hair called attention to spectacular matching earrings. With flushed cheeks and a harried demeanor, she slid into the empty seat beside Chad.

"Sorry I'm late. I couldn't find my bracelet. I could have sworn I'd packed it, but now I'm not so sure."

"Ms. Westbrook," O'Neill said with his usual smooth manners, "this is Erin Fairchild from Palm Beach."

Trish held her breath, then released it with relief when no one queried her about the Fairchilds. She'd picked the name from thin air, not knowing such a Palm Beach family actually existed.

"Hi." Victoria's smile was friendly. She gazed at Trish and her brown eyes widened. "Great dress. I love Versace."

For a second, Trish's mind went blank. Then she realized that Victoria was referring to the second-hand designer gown she'd purchased last year in a consignment shop. "Thanks. Me, too."

Panic was beginning to set in. With O'Neill silent but vigilant on one side and the Averys incommunicado across the table, Trish worried how she'd keep up a conversation without exposing the fact that she didn't belong among these wealthy guests. Her concern soon dissolved under the constant patter of Victoria's words. The woman chatted nonstop about her shopping expedition the previous day to Cashiers and Highlands and monopolized the conversation throughout the main course. Somehow, she managed to eat and talk while displaying impeccable table manners.

When Victoria finally paused for breath, Chad glanced toward the terrace doors. "Any sign of the reporter?"

O'Neill tensed, but said nothing. Trish feigned ignorance. "Reporter?"

"The woman who's missing," Chad said. "She's a reporter for the *Tampa Tribune*."

Victoria made a face. "What's a reporter doing here?" She fixed O'Neill with a look of annoyance. "People expect their privacy at Endless Sky."

"Are you suggesting," O'Neill said mildly, "that I should run background checks on everyone who registers?"

"I don't see why not." Mrs. Avery shifted her attention from her veal piccata and spoke for the first time. Her haughty gaze swept the others at the table before focusing on the resident manager. "You could weed out undesirables that way."

"I know why Debra Devlin is here," Chad announced with a conspiratorial gleam in his eyes.

"Really?" Trish didn't have to fake surprise.

"She's looking for the same person I am," he said.

"And who would that be?" O'Neill's well-modulated voice revealed only the slightest interest.

"Quinn Stevens."

"Mr. Stevens isn't here," O'Neill said.

Chad shrugged. "That's what I'd expect you to say. He owns the place, so he's your boss. If he wanted to stay here incognito, it would be your job to protect his privacy."

"It's my job to protect the privacy of all our guests."

"How do you know this reporter was looking for Quinn Stevens?" Trish asked Chad.

He paused while a waiter served his dessert, flan garnished with a blackberry sauce. "She questioned me. She was convinced Stevens is among the guests, and she was using the process of elimination to find him. She seemed hell-bent on getting an interview with him."

"And why are you looking for Stevens?" O'Neill asked.

Angry color suffused Chad's face. "I have a score to settle with the Last Man Standing."

"A score?" Trish asked.

"Like a duel?" Victoria's eyes blazed with interest. "How exciting!"

"Stevens cheated me in a real estate deal."

The venom in Chad's voice made Trish shiver.

"That's a serious allegation," O'Neill said in his usual calm tone.

"His interference cost me serious money," Chad said with a scowl. "And I intend to make him pay."

Trish turned the conversation back to Debra. If her sister had discovered Stevens, would the man resort to violence to guard his privacy? "But this reporter... had she figured out who Stevens is?"

"If she had, she didn't tell me." Chad drove his spoon into his flan with a fury probably intended for Quinn Stevens.

"O'Neill," Victoria said, apparently tiring of talk of Stevens, "what's on the agenda for tomorrow?"

"A white-water rafting expedition leaves at dawn. And the helicopter will be available to ferry guests into Asheville for the afternoon. There's an arts-and-crafts street festival, with mountain music and clogging demonstrations."

"Will you be our pilot?" Victoria asked.

"Not this time," O'Neill said. "I have other duties tomorrow."

"You fly?" Trish wondered if O'Neill was ex-military, which would explain both his phenomenal build and possibly his taciturn personality.

"Yes."

She waited, expecting more explanation, but O'Neill didn't elaborate.

Instead, he stood and placed his linen napkin on the table beside his untouched dessert. "If you'll excuse me, I must see that the rescue teams have food and drink for themselves and their dogs."

He crossed the room toward the terrace, moving with the grace and confidence of an athlete in superb condition.

Victoria watched him go and sighed. "He's the best-looking man here. And the least approachable. I'm tempted to start a pool among the female guests. First one to be kissed by O'Neill wins."

Mrs. Avery sniffed. "Such vulgarity."

Eyes filled with mischief, Victoria grinned at the old lady. "Does that mean you're in or out?"

In response, Mrs. Avery stood with as much speed and dignity as her old bones allowed and stalked away with her husband trailing in her wake.

"Put your money on kissing me, gorgeous," Chad whispered in Trish's ear, "and you'll win the pool tonight."

"I'm flattered," Trish lied, "but I can't."

"Don't tell me you left your heart in Palm Beach," Chad said. "Who's the lucky man?"

Trish assumed what she hoped was an enigmatic smile and shrugged her shoulders. "Please excuse me. I've had a busy day. I'm going to turn in early."

BACK IN HER SUITE, Trish shed her dress and Aunt Samantha's diamonds for a soft T-shirt and sweatpants. Someone, probably Ludie May, had a fire crackling in the sitting room fireplace. In the bedroom, the covers had been turned down and Godiva chocolates placed on the pillow. A basket on the night table held bottled water and several of the latest bestsellers. But, in spite of the amenities, her suite seemed more foreboding at night. More pronounced than earlier was the sensation that she wasn't alone, a ridiculous notion, she assured herself, since the room was obviously empty.

She recalled Ludie May's warning about spirits, a claim Trish had laughed at in the light of day. Tonight, however, the eerie atmosphere at Endless Sky made anything seem possible.

Too agitated to sleep, Trish opened the balcony doors and stared across the dark silhouettes of rolling ridges that stretched as far as she could see. She remembered reading somewhere that these mountains were more ancient than the Rockies, and, therefore, more worn and less rugged. But beneath the wash of pale moonlight, they appeared rugged enough.

Thoughts of Deb lost in that wilderness were too painful, so Trish picked up the latest Robert Parker mystery and tried to read. After a chapter, unable to concentrate on the printed page, she gave up and turned her mind to O'Neill. The man's mystique had captured her imagination and made her want to know more about him.

Yeah, right. She and every other woman at the resort, she thought, remembering Victoria's fascination. O'Neill probably assumed his enigmatic facade to match the mystical atmosphere that pervaded the resort. He'd no doubt even trained the staff to mention ghosts and American Indian legends to the guests to enhance the effect.

Knowing she needed rest if she planned to hike the trails in search of Deb in the morning, Trish turned off the bedside lamp and scooted beneath the covers. She'd never feared the dark, but the isolation and strange atmosphere of Endless Sky made her jumpy. She debated leaving a light on, then laughed at her own fears. Worry about Deb had made her understandably edgy. There was nothing to fear.

Her head touched the pillows, and a presence brushed her mind.

She bolted upright, heart pounding. *Deb, are you here? Talk to me!*

When no one answered, Ludie May's references to Cherokee ghosts flooded her thoughts, and her eyes searched the shadows cast by the moonlight streaming through the balcony doors.

Trish saw no one, but the presence in her mind remained.

Who are you? she insisted, shivering with uneasiness.

No one replied.

She shook her head in a futile attempt to throw off the intrusion into her thoughts. Her racing pulse ratcheted up several notches and her breathing quickened.

It's this place, she thought. *It's doing a number on my imagination.*

I am not your imagination, a male voice that sounded ancient, wise and weary spoke in her head. *Do not be afraid. I am a friend.*

Who are you? Trish repeated.

But the presence was gone, and the only sound left in the room was the soft keening of the wind beneath the eaves.

Chapter Four

O'Neill was up before dawn after only a few hours of sleep. He took a quick shower, pulled on jeans, hiking boots and a sweater, and stepped outside onto the porch of the manager's cottage. In the valley that stretched along the north side of the ridge, low clouds, remnants of yesterday's rain, streamed like blown scarves. The cold, clear autumn air carried the pungent tang of wood smoke, and the mouth-watering aroma of baking cinnamon buns wafted from the resort's kitchen.

He left the porch, climbed the trail that led from the cluster of staff residences, which had been built below the ridgeline to hide them from the main building's view, and trudged toward the wide swath of now-ruined lawn. The sheriff's department, which was coordinating the hunt for Debra Devlin, had erected a command tent at the edge of the drive. The search, judging from the number of empty vehicles parked nearby, was ongoing.

O'Neill stepped inside the tent and was pleased to find his staff had followed his instructions from the night before. A serving table had been set, complete with thermal jugs of hot coffee and tea, cold orange juice, baskets of fresh fruit and an enormous platter of pastries, bagels and granola bars.

Captain Metcalf, the uniformed officer monitoring radio communications at a nearby desk, nodded in greeting. Short and powerfully built, his middle-aged face had the weathered look of a man who'd spent most of his life outdoors. If he was typical of many of the locals O'Neill had met, he'd rather be bear hunting now than searching for a lost reporter.

"Any sign of her?" O'Neill asked.

The officer, who'd been on duty when O'Neill left the tent last night, shook his head. "We've done a grid search with the chopper, working outward from the resort. Nothing's shown up on our thermal sensors but small nocturnal animals and one large hit that turned out to be a bear."

"What about the teams on the ground? Have they found anything?"

His eyes tired, Metcalf shook his head again. "A bloodhound picked up a scent on the trail where the cell phone was found, but lost it in less than a mile. The rains have washed away most traces." He sighed and rubbed the back of his neck. "It's about time to call in the cadaver dogs."

"You think she's dead?" The bad news hit O'Neill hard. As manager of the resort, he felt a responsibility for his missing guest. As a human being, he mourned the loss of an attractive, vibrant young woman who'd been a breath of fresh air among the usual pompous clientele.

Metcalf shrugged. "The local television

stations have been broadcasting her photo and asking anyone who's seen her to give them a call."

"No response?"

"Oh, we've had calls, all right. Somebody spotted her in Weaverville."

"Did you check it out?"

Metcalf smiled for the first time, adding even more wrinkles to the lines of his face. "She was seen at a convenience store in a pink Cadillac. With Elvis." His expression sobered. "None of the other reports panned out, either. My guess is the woman wandered deep into the wilderness and either became lost or fell at one of the overlooks. Either way, between yesterday's heavy rains and last night's drop in temperature, if she's out in the open, her chances for survival don't look good."

"Any reason to expect foul play?" O'Neill asked with reluctance. "I have other guests whose safety is my responsibility."

Metcalf rose, stretched and poured himself a cup of coffee. "At this point, we can't rule out anything. Your guests should use caution. Travel in pairs if they're hiking. Better still, take a guide if they're wandering far from the resort."

"Has her family been notified?"

"The Tampa FBI office is keeping them informed of our progress. Or, I should say, lack of it."

"Anything else you need here?"

"Luck, and lots of it. We're looking for a needle in a haystack."

On that grim note, O'Neill left the command tent, crossed the dew-slick lawn in the thin gray light and entered the dining room from the terrace. Five of the guests, including Victoria Westbrook and Chad Englewood, were having breakfast before starting out on their white-water rafting expedition. Judd Raye would drive them to their starting point on the East Pigeon River, then pick them up downstream later in the day.

O'Neill nodded in greeting, poured himself a mug of coffee at the buffet table and headed toward his office. Inside, he raised the blinds, and the first rays of morning light flooded his desk. He settled into his chair and turned his thoughts from Debra Devlin to the woman who'd kept him awake most of the night.

He'd been caught off guard by the effect Erin Fairchild had had on him, and he'd lain sleepless, attempting to analyze her impact. After Alicia's treachery and several years at Endless Sky, O'Neill had thought himself immune to the beautiful, rich women who moved in and out of his life like the tides of the ocean. But Erin Fairchild had caught him up like a rip current that wouldn't let go.

Last night at dinner, she'd stunned him, turning his original assessment of her upside down and inside out. After picking Erin up at the airport and having lunch with her, O'Neill had concluded she wasn't wealthy but more likely someone who'd robbed her savings or hocked her car to come to Endless Sky to escape some major disappointment in her life.

When she'd shown up at dinner, wearing enough diamonds to open her own branch of Cartier and dressed in designer black velvet, he'd had to reevaluate his original conclusions. Desire flooded him at the memory of that dress. With its high neckline that showcased her impressive diamond necklace, long tight sleeves and a hem short enough to reveal amazingly long legs, the dress, in covering her up, had called attention to Erin's attributes: a waist he could probably span with his hands and perfectly proportioned breasts and hips. Dangling diamond earrings, along with stray curls from her upswept blond hair, had emphasized the slender column of her throat. The woman had been drop-dead gorgeous, all right. No wonder that jerk, Chad Englewood, had practically salivated over her all evening.

But her appearance alone wasn't all that had changed. At the airport, throughout the ride back and at lunch in her suite, Erin had seemed off-kilter, slightly ditzy, as if having trouble establishing her emotional equilibrium. At dinner, however, she'd seemed perfectly at ease, withstanding even the withering condescension of Violet Avery with poise and grace.

So which woman was the *real* Erin Fairchild? And why was he spending so much time thinking about her? To avoid the harsh reality of Debra Devlin's disappearance? That had to be the reason. He'd decided years ago to disengage his emotions where wealthy, pretty women were concerned and saw no reason to break his rule now. Pushing Erin Fairchild from his mind, he shoved back from his desk, grabbed his empty mug and went back to the dining room for a refill.

The rafting party had departed. The only people remaining in the dining room were Henry, the sous-chef, who manned the omelet station at the breakfast buffet—and Erin, who sat alone at a table by the window, staring outside.

Get your coffee, go back to the office, he told himself, *and leave the woman alone.*

Ignoring her, try as he might, was impossible. He couldn't take his eyes off her. Her expressive hands were wrapped around a mug of steaming coffee and her mournful gaze was fixed on the command tent on the lawn. He wouldn't have thought it possible, but she looked even more beautiful this morning, despite the aura of sadness that enveloped her.

O'Neill refilled his cup and approached her table, wondering which facet of Erin he'd encounter today—wealthy bombshell, ditzy blonde or some new incarnation? "Mind if I join you?"

Caught by surprise, she flinched and sloshed hot coffee over her hands.

He grabbed a linen napkin from an adjacent place setting, dipped it in her glass of ice water and quickly bathed her hands where the steaming liquid had touched them. She had long, slender fingers and well-manicured, natural nails with pale half-moon crescents at their base. Her skin was soft and warm, and her hands seemed small and fragile in his.

Henry, who'd witnessed the accident, appeared at the table with a hand towel, which he gave O'Neill before returning to the omelet station.

"Let me have a look at those fingers," O'Neill said.

With a barely concealed grimace, Erin straightened out her fingers. The skin, especially on her right hand, was an angry red. He gently patted her fingers dry with the towel. "Does that hurt?"

"Just a little. But the sting is going away." Her eyes teared, belying her words.

"I have some burn ointment—"

"Never mind," Erin said. "I'll be fine."

"Ointment will kill the pain."

"It doesn't hurt. Really. The ice water did the trick."

Under the same circumstances, most of his other guests would be indulging in histrionics or threatening to sue. Erin seemed almost apologetic, as if she'd caused the trouble.

O'Neill mopped up the excess coffee and water and handed her half-empty cup and the wet linens to the busboy hovering at his elbow. Following his ingrained training, the teen whisked away the soiled tablecloth and quickly recovered and reset the table.

After the busboy left, O'Neill slid into the chair opposite Erin.

"Impressive," she said with a smile that did strange things to his insides.

"What?"

"The speed of the service around here."

He lifted his cup in a salute. "We aim to please."

A waiter appeared with a fresh mug for Erin. "May I bring you something from the buffet table, ma'am?"

She shook her head. "No, thanks. Just coffee."

The waiter nodded and withdrew.

"Did you miss the van for the rafting party?" O'Neill asked.

Erin took a tentative sip of her coffee as if testing its heat. "I plan to hike this morning."

O'Neill noted her clothes. Usually his guests hit the trails looking as if they'd been outfitted by L.L. Bean's top-of-the-line. Erin wore faded jeans with a matching jacket, a white turtleneck sweater and slightly scuffed running shoes, a complete contradiction to the high-fashion woman who'd graced his table at dinner last night. She'd pulled her blond hair through the expansion hole of her matching denim soft cap, and the result made her appear as young and vulnerable as a teenager.

"Captain Metcalf recommends that no one hike alone," O'Neill warned.

"I won't stray from the main trails."

"It's better to have an escort, under the circumstances."

The look she gave him was bleak, and he noted for the first time the smudges of fatigue under her brilliant seawater eyes. "The missing reporter?"

He nodded.

"Did the rescue squad find anything last night?"

O'Neill provided a brief rundown of Metcalf's report. "You'll probably be perfectly safe hiking, but, since I planned to spend this morning on the trails anyway, why don't you come with me?"

She shook her head. "Thanks, but I prefer my own company today."

He studied her closely, struck by her underlying sadness, laced with a sense of desperation. She shouldn't be alone on unfamiliar trails in her frame of mind. Distracted by her problems, whatever they were, she might become disoriented and lost, or fall and injure herself. He wasn't going to lose another guest. Especially not this one, who had touched a chord deep in a place he thought he had locked safely away from all intrusions.

"You don't want me to lose my job, do you?" he asked.

She frowned. "What do you mean?"

He shrugged. "The sheriff warned me not to let guests hike alone. If anything were to happen to you, it would be my fault, and my boss would have my hide, right before he hands me my walking papers."

"Nothing's going to happen to me," she insisted.

"That's probably what Debra Devlin thought."

Erin tilted her head upward so that the steady gaze of her blue-green eyes hit him full force from beneath the bill of her soft cap. She was silent for a long moment. "Okay, you can come with me on one condition."

He grinned. "You do that a lot?"

"What?"

"Set your own conditions?"

Her expression turned puzzled.

"You wouldn't let me order your lunch yesterday unless I ate with you," he reminded her.

"What's the point of being rich if you can't set your own rules?" Her delectable lips turned upward in a ghost of a smile.

"So what's the condition du jour?" Erin had been flirting with him yesterday with her demands. He found himself looking forward to more flirtation, but her response wasn't what he expected.

"I want to help search for the missing reporter." Erin's trace of a smile vanished, and her expression and voice turned solemn. "Can you show me the trail where her cell phone was found?"

"That's almost a full day's hike, round-trip."

O'Neill wasn't about to divulge that she'd just suggested the route he'd planned to cover on his own. The rescue teams had already searched there, but after five years of living on the mountain and walking its trails, he knew the area better than anyone. It was, after all, his own backyard, and if anything along the trail was amiss, he'd be the one most likely to spot it.

With five of the guests off on a rafting expedition and the others signed up for the trip to Asheville this afternoon, he wouldn't be needed at the resort for the rest of the day. He'd planned to scour the area where the cell phone had been located and return in time to play his usual role as host at dinner.

"I don't have any other plans for today," Erin said. "A full day's hike is no problem."

As much as he would enjoy her company, he feared she'd only slow him down. "You'll miss the festival in Asheville. There's room for one more in the chopper."

The color left her face at his suggestion, and he remembered her fear of heights that he'd noted yesterday.

"I don't like crowds," she said.

He cast about for another excuse to dissuade her. "You'll miss lunch."

She laughed and shook her head. "I saw the lunches the kitchen prepared for the rafting party. Your chef over there could whip up a couple more in minutes."

O'Neill still couldn't put a finger on what made this extraordinary woman tick. "Why are you so determined to go hiking?"

"To enjoy the scenery and mountain air."

He shook his head. "You could do that sitting in a rocker on the porch. Why are you so interested in searching for Debra Devlin?"

A sudden stillness settled over Erin and she was silent for a moment before answering. "If I were lost and alone in these mountains, I'd want everyone possible looking for me. Wouldn't you?"

She was a constant source of amazement. Most of the guests at Endless Sky were accustomed to having the world revolve around them, and their huge fortunes were the grease that facilitated that rotation.

Erin's empathy was a pleasant and unexpected change from such self-absorption.

"I'll have Henry pack our lunches," he said, "and I'll meet you on the back terrace in fifteen minutes."

WAITING FOR O'NEILL, Trish stood on the terrace and tried not to appear too anxious. She'd already raised the resident manager's suspicions by insisting on joining the search, so she'd have to proceed with caution. She stretched out her hands where the coffee had burned them, but the angry red splotches had disappeared, along with the pain. All that remained was the memory of O'Neill's firm, warm touch and the concern in his eyes. Having a handsome man fussing over her had been a new and heady experience.

Forget it. Taking care of the guests is his job. You shouldn't read anything into it.

She drew in a deep breath of cool air and surveyed her surroundings. In the bright clear light of morning, Endless Sky had lost its brooding aspect, making her believe she must have dreamed the voice that had spoken in her mind the night before. It hadn't returned, and exhaustion from worrying over Deb and keeping up the charade as a wealthy guest had plunged Trish into a deep, restful sleep. She felt energized this morning. And hopeful. If Deb was out there and Trish could get close enough, the sisters would make psychic contact. Then she could lead the rescue teams to Debra.

Hang on, Deb. I'm coming.

She heard no reply.

"All set?" O'Neill stepped out of the dining room. He slung a rucksack over his back and handed her one of two hefty, carved wooden walking sticks. "You'll need this to steady you on some of the steeper patches."

He looked askance at her running shoes. His own footwear was a pair of sturdy boots, but she hadn't had time to purchase proper hiking gear. Her sneakers would have to do.

He pointed in the direction of the sun

that had risen just above the eastern mountains. "The trail takes off on the other side of the drive."

Trish hefted her walking stick and fell into step beside him, and he shortened his stride so she could keep up. O'Neill looked different this morning, still mysterious but not quite as foreboding without his black wardrobe. His jeans and beige sweater, with suede patches on the shoulders and elbows, although obviously high quality and very expensive, gave him a more casual appearance and made him seem almost approachable.

"O'Neill?" she said.

"Yes."

"Do you have a first name?"

"Not one that I answer to." He swept aside a rhododendron branch that blocked the entrance to the path. "My parents didn't consult me before branding me with a name I hate. O'Neill is all I need."

She brushed against him as he cleared the trail for her, and his scent swirled on the morning mist, enveloping her in an aura of musk and balsam. For an instant, longing flooded her, a desire to feel the strength of his arms around her, to hear that deep, rich voice murmur in her ear, to feel his lips on hers.

The unexpected rush of desire stopped her in her tracks and left her struggling to breathe. What was wrong with her? Her sister was missing, and she was indulging in romantic fantasies when she should be concentrating on the search.

"You okay?" O'Neill slipped his arm around her.

She fought the impulse to lean into his embrace. Instead, she straightened her shoulders and shook off his arm. "I'm just a little winded."

"It's the altitude." His voice was kind, filled with concern that made him even harder to resist. "We'll slow our pace until you're acclimated."

Acclimated, Trish thought with a shiver of panic. The more time she spent with O'Neill, the more attractive he became. She doubted she'd ever accustom herself to such charm. "I'm okay. Let's keep moving."

The trail took them along the top of the ridge, a barren sweep of rocks and boulders broken only by scattered low shrubs, bright with red fall foliage, their branches gnarled and twisted by the constant wind. Trish kept her eyes on the trail to avoid the dizzying vistas on either side. In the shimmering morning air, a quick glimpse had revealed folds of blue mountains stretching in every direction, as if she was standing on top of the world. Her fear of heights kicked in, and only the comforting breadth of the ridge's top path kept a panic attack at bay.

The trail was wide enough for O'Neill to walk beside her and she plied him with questions to keep her mind off the heights they were traversing.

"I read on the resort's Web site that you're only open June through October," she said. "How come? Endless Sky seems the perfect spot for a Christmas vacation. I can picture a huge lighted tree in the lobby by the fireplace."

Her nerves had her babbling like the river the others were rafting on this morning.

"The parkway's closed most of the winter," he explained. "The weather's too brutal for hiking and rafting, or for counting on the Hummer and helicopter for access. And we have no ski facilities. Most of our clients would rather go elsewhere in winter."

"Where do you go?"

"My boss also owns a resort in St. Thomas. I help out there while Endless Sky is closed."

"Winter in the Caribbean," she said with an envious smile. "Must be tough."

"It's a nasty job, but somebody has to do it." He stopped and looked back. "You have a great view of the resort from here."

Trish turned and looked back at the hotel, outlined against the brilliant blue sky, and imagined the resort in winter, windows shuttered, the entire structure shrouded in clouds and buffeted by icy winds. The prospect made her shudder. "Nobody stays over the winter?"

"Depends on how you define nobody." He pivoted and began walking again. "The ghosts never leave."

Chapter Five

"Ghosts?" Trish hurried to keep up. "You're kidding, right?"

He shook his head, and his midnight-blue eyes were somber. "No, I'm not kidding. I didn't believe in the supernatural before coming to Endless Sky. Now I'm not so sure."

"You've *seen* these ghosts?" His comment made her reassess the voice she'd heard in her room the previous night. Maybe it hadn't been a dream.

"Specific entities?" He shook his head. "But I've seen things I can't explain."

"Like what?"

"The Brown Mountain lights."

Her fear of heights momentarily overridden by talk of ghosts, she scanned the surrounding ridges. "Which one is Brown Mountain?"

"You can't see it from here. It's north of Asheville, near Blowing Rock." He pointed north and the sun struck his profile, illuminating the classic lines of his face.

"What's supernatural about lights on a mountain?" She wondered if he was teasing her. "Highways and railroads run through these hills. Someone's bound to observe headlights occasionally."

"That was my first reaction, too, but these lights were seen by the Cherokee centuries before the invention of cars and trains. Even before the advent of electric lights."

Trish remained skeptical. "What do these Brown Mountain lights look like?"

"Huge glowing balls, sometimes exploding high above the mountain like Roman candles, but without sound." He glanced at her without a hint of teasing, his eyes dark and serious. "When I saw them, they rose slowly and gradually faded away."

"There has to be a scientific explanation," she insisted. "Decaying vegetation, Saint Elmo's fire."

He shook his head. "They've been investigated by the U.S. Meteorological Society and the U.S. Geological Survey, and by other independent scientists. No one's been able to come up with a definitive cause."

"Okay, I'll bite. What's the supernatural explanation?"

"The Cherokees reported seeing these lights as far back as the year 1200. Prior to that, a terrible battle between the Cherokee and Catawba tribes was fought near Brown Mountain." O'Neill's voice was matter-of-fact, but his words made the hair on the back of her neck stand on end. "The Cherokee believe the lights are torches, carried by the spirits of Indian women, searching over the centuries for their lost husbands and sweethearts."

"Makes a good story, at least." Trish suppressed a shudder.

"That's only one story. These mountains are filled with Cherokee legends and tales of Tar Heel ghosts. Sometimes I can almost feel them, even if I can't see them." With his dark good looks, O'Neill looked like someone out of a legend himself, a man with a story, a man with secrets. A dangerous man.

Trish wished she'd bothered to tell someone else at the resort where she was going and with whom. But she shook off her gloomy thoughts. O'Neill's tales of Cherokee spirits had spooked her, but surely she had no reason to fear the man who'd been so kind to her.

They had reached a saddle in the ridge, and the trail plunged downward into an eerie stand of dead evergreens, a forest of botanical ghosts.

"Did a fire kill these trees?" she asked. Their gray skeletons were covered with moss and lichens, making them appear ancient and sad.

O'Neill shook his head. "Pollution and acid rain."

Voices sounded ahead. Trish and O'Neill rounded a curve in the descending trail and a trio of hikers approached, one holding the lead of a German shepherd. Two of the men, tall and slightly built with freckled complexions and pale blue eyes, looked like brothers. The third was short and swarthy. All three wore the distinctive neon-orange windbreakers and soft caps of the rescue squad. The dog wore a working harness and a vest embroidered with the squad's name.

O'Neill greeted them. "Find anything?"

Trish held her breath and hoped for good news.

The short man shook his head. "We've been out all night, following this trail all the way to Pisgah Point. We found zip."

"The dog didn't pick up a scent?" she asked.

The handler shook his head.

"I thought bloodhounds were used for tracking." Erin patted the friendly shepherd's head.

"Heidi is trained for tracking, too, but she's best at maneuvering into spaces a person would have trouble reaching, like under fallen trees, down steep slopes or into small burrows." The man scratched behind the dog's ears. "Heidi checked everywhere, but never gave us an alert."

"Does that mean the missing woman didn't come this way?" Trish asked.

The handler shook his head again and spoke in his slow drawl with a mountain twang. "She could have. There's still a lot of country we haven't covered. It's like looking for a needle in a field of haystacks."

"Breakfast is waiting back at the resort," O'Neill said. "I appreciate your efforts."

"We'll rest up and head out again," the short man said.

Trish and O'Neill moved off the path for them to pass.

"These mountain folk are good people," O'Neill said as soon as the men had moved out of earshot. "Except for a few sheriff's deputies, everyone on the search-and-rescue teams is a volunteer."

"If they've already covered this trail, shouldn't we look somewhere else?"

O'Neill nodded. "There's a fork up

ahead. The right path goes to Pisgah Point, the other to the place where the cell phone was found. We'll search the left fork."

At the fork in the trail, they descended farther down the ridge into a forest of deciduous trees, their foliage brilliant with fall color. The narrow path was treacherously slick with a layer of dead leaves, wet from yesterday's rains. Trish was glad for the walking stick to help keep her balance. They followed the trail deeper into the woods, and, ahead of her, O'Neill peered through the trees and underbrush on either side. She was struck again by their isolation and her vulnerability, alone in the wilderness with a stranger. But she would risk her own safety to find Deb.

"There're dozens of smaller trails leading off from this one," he explained. "I'm looking for broken branches, strips of cloth, any sign of someone having left this trail recently."

"Who made all these paths?" Trish asked. "Hikers?"

"These trails are almost as old as the

mountains themselves. Most were bear trails, which the Indians used for hunting. Now they're used for recreation."

"Bears?" she said in alarm. "Are there bears around here?"

"I doubt we'll see them. They hide in the trees and generally avoid people."

Trish cast a worried glance at the canopy of the trees high above her. Yellow, gold and red leaves shimmered in the breeze, but she saw no sign of bears.

Thrusting everything from her mind but her sister, she reached out with her thoughts. *Deb, if you're here, talk to me.*

She stopped and stiffened as something brushed her mind.

Deb?

But the sensation passed, and Deb didn't answer.

Are you here, Deb? It's me, Trish.

She scanned the area surrounding the path for some sign of her sister's having been there, but found nothing.

"Something wrong?" O'Neill called from lower on the trail. "Find anything?"

Stalling for time, she shook her head and bent down and pretended to tie her shoe. *Deb?*

Receiving no answer, Trish hurried to catch up with O'Neill. Even in her worry over Deb, she couldn't help but notice how handsome her guide was. He looked every inch the outdoorsman as he strode confidently down the path. The muscles of his thighs and calves rippled beneath the snug fit of his jeans as he moved sure-footedly over the rugged terrain. Dappled sunlight, peeking through the overhanging trees, illuminated his sleek dark hair and the chiseled angles of his face.

O'Neill to the rescue, she thought with a smile. What woman wouldn't feel safe in those powerful arms? Or was that prospect of safety an illusion? Shaking away her preoccupation with O'Neill, she concentrated on looking for her sister.

The steep trail wound downward until it crossed a rock-strewn creek. On the other side, the well-worn path led up a steep slope. Trish's sneakers slipped on the damp humus, and several times she would have fallen if O'Neill hadn't grabbed her and hoisted her beside him. For someone whose job kept him behind a hotel desk, he had amazing strength and apparently unlimited lung capacity. He wasn't even breathing hard.

Trish, however, wasn't in such good shape. By the time they reached level ground at the top of the next ridge, her chest was heaving with exertion and the muscles of her legs trembled from the unaccustomed strain. She wanted to find Deb, but she couldn't take another step without resting first.

As if reading her mind, O'Neill announced, "Time for lunch."

He swept fallen leaves from a wide flat rock beside the trail and poked around its base with his walking stick.

"What are you doing?" she asked.

"Checking for timber rattlers."

She shuddered and prayed her sister hadn't been snake bitten. "Bears, snakes. Any other hazards I should be wary of?"

With a grin, he pointed his walking stick to a plant on the opposite side of the trail. "Only poison ivy."

"Thanks for the warning." Grateful for the opportunity to rest her quivering muscles, she sank onto one edge of the flat rock.

O'Neill shifted the rucksack from his back to the rock, sat alongside her and dug into the pack's depths to remove thermal containers. Within minutes, he had a feast spread on a burgundy linen cloth between them.

Trish, whose idea of a picnic was of a bucket of fried chicken, a liter of soda and a roll of paper towels, struggled not to gawk at the crusty croissants filled with almond chicken salad, a compote of baked apples with raisins in cinnamon sauce and glasses for the chilled white wine. Not a paper plate or plastic utensil in sight.

Reminding herself that a Palm Beach heiress would accept the extraordinary meal as common, she reached for a sandwich. "I'm starved."

"It's the mountain air. And the exercise." O'Neill took a croissant for himself. "So," he said, after swallowing his first bite, "what do you do when you're not traveling?"

Trish bit into her sandwich to give herself an opportunity to think. She'd been so concerned about Deb, she hadn't taken time to concoct a complete cover story. Now, she figured the closer she kept to the truth, the more convincing she'd be. "I volunteer at a local middle school."

He gazed at her with raised eyebrows and a hint of disbelief. "Middle school? Isn't that a tough age to work with?"

"I love the challenge." She hoped whoever was covering her classes was up to the task. "Two of the boys I mentor have learning disabilities—dyslexia and attention deficit disorder. I get a lot of satisfaction from helping them improve their study skills."

O'Neill's gaze locked on her, and she forced herself not to squirm beneath the scrutiny of those deep, dark eyes. He reached for a linen napkin, lifted it to her face and gently dabbed at the corner of her mouth.

"Mayonnaise," he explained.

His touch rattled her, but not nearly so

much as the question that followed. "Who are you?"

"What?"

A cold wind ruffled the linen tablecloth, and the chill cut through her layers of clothing and made her shiver. She was intensely aware of the vulnerability of her situation, alone in the wilderness with a man she barely knew. Did O'Neill know more about what had happened to Deb than he'd let on? Even more frightening was the possibility that he might have been responsible in some way for her sister's disappearance. He was Quinn Stevens's employee. How far would Stevens go to protect his privacy?

Trish pushed away her fears. Tales of evil spirits, ghosts and strange lights had affected her reason. O'Neill had been the epitome of kindness and consideration since their first meeting. She had no reason to fear him.

She hoped.

"I'm not sure what you're asking," she said.

His crooked smile magnified his appeal.

"You're unlike any woman I've ever met. Every time I think I have you figured out, you surprise me."

Remembering her charade as a man-hunting playgirl, she slanted her head, batted her eyelashes and flashed a coy grin. "I've been told men like a sense of mystery in women."

For a second, she worried that flirtation with a strange man in the middle of nowhere wasn't exactly smart, but her fears proved groundless when her playful come-on did nothing to rouse O'Neill's ardor. If anything, he seemed put off by her ploy.

"Finish your lunch," he ordered. "We should start back."

She ate a few more bites, but what little appetite she'd had was gone, squelched by worry for Deb. She wondered if her sister was hungry, cold, hurt—

Beware. The ancient voice from last night's dream sounded in her head.

Trish dropped her wineglass, shattering it on the rock, and jumped to her feet. *Who are you?*

"What's wrong?" O'Neill had sprung

from his seat beside her. "Did something bite you?"

She shook her head, unable to think of an excuse for her bizarre behavior.

"Are you okay?" O'Neill asked.

The sincerity in his voice and the kindness in his expression almost undid her. The voice she longed to hear most of all remained silent, and she didn't know whether the spirit who had spoken was good or evil. Whatever it was, she wouldn't let it deter her from her search. "We should keep going."

"Why? Did you spot something?"

She shook her head.

O'Neill started packing the remnants of their lunch into his rucksack. "That's a tough climb up that next ridge, even steeper than it looks. It's another hour at least to the top."

"So?"

He pointed across the gorge where the creek ran to the path that led back to the resort. "That's also an uphill climb. It'll take twice as long to go up as it did coming down. Even if we head back now, we'll be pushing it to make it back by dark."

"You go on back. I'll continue alone." Her sister might be out there, and Trish wasn't going to abandon her.

"I can't let you do that," O'Neill said firmly and with irritating reason. "I don't want another missing woman on my hands." He grasped her shoulders and the warmth from his hands seeped through her jacket. "The rescue squad can check out this trail."

"But—"

"Look, even if we found Debra," he said with maddening reason, "if she's fallen from the trail—which would have to be the case since this path's been searched at least once already—it'll take special skills and equipment that we don't have to retrieve her."

From the firmness of his grip and the strength of his reasoning, Trish realized further argument was futile. She reached out with her mind. *Deb, are you here?*

But Deb didn't answer.

Trish heaved a sigh and conceded to O'Neill's demands. "We'd better hurry, then. I'd rather not be out here when night falls," she said.

But O'Neill didn't release her. He stood for a long, intense moment, gazing into her eyes, as if searching for answers she couldn't give him. His breath, fragrant with cinnamon, was warm upon her face, triggering responses in all her senses. The man was a rock, and she suppressed once again her desire to throw herself against his chest and seek shelter in his arms.

She felt bereft when he finally dropped his hands from her shoulders, but she stifled her feelings. She needed all her emotional energy to try to establish contact with Deb.

Turning back the way they'd come, she scrambled down the steep incline toward the creek.

BY THE TIME she and O'Neill neared Endless Sky, the sun had set beyond the western mountains and the light of the full moon bathed the ridgetop, lighting the last steps of their journey.

The hotel, aglow inside and out, loomed in the distance like a beacon.

Trish hurried her steps, but was drawn up short by a presence in her mind.

Trish, are you there? Deb's voice was weak, but unmistakable.

Yes, where are you?

I'm not sure. Somewhere on the trail.

I'm coming.

Trish turned back the way they'd come.

"What are you doing?" O'Neill asked.

Trish considered her options. She could spend time arguing with O'Neill. Maybe even try to convince him of the psychic connection she had with Debra. But recalling the disbelief she had encountered in the past when she'd had the courage to broach the subject of her shared communication with Debra with a third party, she realized she'd only be wasting time. Her best bet was to dump O'Neill and return to Debra on her own.

"I just needed a rest." Trish turned back

toward Endless Sky and forced her weary muscles to hurry. The sooner she could reach the resort and lose O'Neill, the sooner she could return to the trail and Deb.

Within minutes, they were crossing the resort's broad lawn.

"I'll go to my room to change for dinner," she said as they climbed to the terrace. She intended to backtrack as soon as she was out of O'Neill's sight. Maybe in her desperation, she'd only imagined Deb's voice, but she couldn't ignore the real chance that Deb was still alive and calling for help.

"No need to change," he said, spoiling her plans. "Tonight's casual night. We're serving barbecue on the front porch."

Before she could think of an excuse to leave, he took her elbow and guided her through the dining room and lobby and onto the wide covered porch that ran the full length of the resort. Cheerful paper lanterns had been hung along the eaves, tables with red-checkered cloths were scattered across the porch's broad expanse and a small band, composed of a fiddler and two guitar players, cranked out a lively mountain tune.

Guests helped themselves to barbecued ribs, corn on the cob and coleslaw at the buffet tables before choosing their seats.

"Erin!" Victoria Westbrook, dressed in tight designer jeans, a Western shirt spangled with rhinestones and tooled leather boots, waved from the buffet table. "Join me."

"Go ahead," O'Neill said. "I'll get rid of this rucksack."

"And alert the rescue squad to check that trail?"

"Sure," he said, but he didn't sound sure.

He probably thought her behavior earlier on the mountain eccentric at best, nuts at worst. But the sooner she could escape his watchful eye, the sooner she could continue the search on her own.

Waiting for O'Neill to disappear, Trish crossed the room, snagged a bottle of water at the beverage station, and joined Victoria, who was ladling enough food onto her plate to feed a small army.

"You go, girl," Victoria said with a teasing grin. "Rumor has it you spent the day with O'Neill."

"We were looking for the missing reporter."

"Yeah, right." Victoria winked.

"What else would I be doing?" Trish demanded, irritated by the woman's innuendo.

"What every woman who's ever stayed at Endless Sky wants to do. Seduce that untouchable, unapproachable, delectable man."

Trish watched the handsome resident manager as he worked his way across the porch, speaking with guests, instructing the staff. "So he's that much of a lady-killer?"

Victoria snorted. "I wish. The man's notorious for avoiding women like the plague. He never gets involved with the guests, no matter how hard some of us have thrown ourselves at him. That's why your accomplishment is such a coup."

"I didn't accomplish anything," Trish insisted. "We just went hiking."

Victoria considered her between narrowed eyes. "Too bad, if you're telling the truth."

"Why wouldn't I?"

"Girl, nobody at this place is truthful. Everybody's putting on an act."

Trish's senses went on immediate alert. Had Deb uncovered secrets someone hadn't wanted brought to light, especially by a member of the media? Secrets someone had wanted to make certain she wouldn't tell? Trish returned Victoria's narrowed gaze. "What's *your* act?"

Victoria nodded toward a table in the far corner of the porch, and they threaded their way around the other tables toward it. The state of Trish's muscles informed her that she needed a few minutes off her feet before tackling the trails again.

Once they were seated, Victoria leaned toward Trish. "My secret is that I hate this place."

"Then why are you here?"

"To get away from my mother." Victoria sighed dramatically and chomped into her ear of corn. "She runs my life. She's even picked out the man I'm supposed to marry."

"You're a grown woman," Trish said. "Why don't you just leave home?"

"The ties that bind," Victoria answered with a grimace and wiped her butter-stained fingers on a red-and-white checkered napkin.

Trish, her thoughts on escaping as soon as her leg muscles stopped trembling, frowned. "I don't understand."

"Mother's money. If I don't jump through her hoops, she cuts off my very hefty allowance."

"Ever thought of earning your own money?" Trish couldn't imagine a life without work.

"How?" Victoria dismissed the idea with a wave of her fingers, flashing gold and jeweled rings in the lantern light. "I've graduated from the world's best finishing school, but I'm not trained for anything, except living well."

She looked so dejected that Trish

couldn't help feeling sorry for her. "Finishing school? In Europe?"

Victoria nodded.

"How many languages do you speak?"

"Five."

"Get a job as a translator."

Victoria scowled. "I'd rather find a husband whom I love madly and who can keep me in the style I'm accustomed to."

At Victoria's lack of initiative, Trish's sympathy evaporated. Trish scanned the gathering of guests. The man who'd sat beside her at dinner the night before had just entered the buffet line. "What about Chad Englewood? I understand he's single."

"That jerk?" Victoria broke a fluffy biscuit in half and took a bite. Her plight apparently hadn't spoiled her appetite. "I don't know how he affords this place. He lost all his money in bad real estate investments."

Chad's comments from the previous night echoed in Trish's mind. Maybe Deb's disappearance had made her paranoid, but she couldn't help wondering if Chad hated Stevens enough to cause an ugly incident at his resort. "He was cheated by Quinn Stevens?"

"So he claims," Victoria said. "More likely his bad fortune is the result of his own incompetence. I'd rather be poor and single than married to such a loser."

"Tell me about the others."

"Others?"

"The ones here putting on acts," Trish prodded.

"Take the Averys, for instance."

"The old couple from Atlanta?"

Victoria nodded. "They come from old money, but it's dwindling fast. They scrimp and save all year to afford a couple weeks at Endless Sky, just so Violet can turn up her nose at the nouveau riche."

Trish blinked in surprise. The haughty Averys were actually poor? The situation at the resort really wasn't what it seemed.

"I feel sorry for them then," Trish said. "It can't be easy being elderly and hard up, especially if you haven't been accustomed to making ends meet all your life. And Mr. Avery seems like a nice man."

"He's okay, but she's a bitch. Speaking of which, see that dark-haired woman at the bar?" Victoria continued.

Trish nodded.

"She's another reporter."

"How do you know?"

"Her name is Tiffany Slocum. I've seen her covering social events in Newport, where she's famous for gate-crashing. She's here for the same reason the missing woman was, to track down and interview Quinn Stevens."

An unscrupulous reporter might go too far to eliminate her competition. The nasty suspicion reminded Trish of her mission. She'd rested long enough.

"Excuse me," she said to Victoria, "I need to clean up before I eat. See you later?"

Victoria, her mouth filled with fried chicken, nodded and waved her away.

Suppressing the urge to bolt, Trish sauntered casually past the dancing couples on the porch.

"Hey, gorgeous, dance with me." Chad

appeared beside her, grabbed her by the arm and swung her toward him.

He didn't seem the type who'd be easily discouraged, so she stifled the impulse to shake him off with a glare. Instead, she flashed a fake smile. "Great. As soon as I get back from the little girls' room."

He released her arm. "I'll be waiting."

Don't hold your breath.

She hurried through the deserted lobby to the elevator and kept a lookout for O'Neill, afraid he might guess her intentions and stop her if he spotted her. Grateful that the elevator door slid open the moment she pushed the Up indicator, she scooted inside and pressed the button for her floor.

Suddenly, she felt someone staring at her back. But when she whipped around, the elevator was empty. Its lights flickered and dimmed, and for a brief moment, it stopped its upward movement before starting again. A power brownout?

Or something more sinister?

The third-floor hall was deserted when

she stepped off the elevator, but with her imagination casting danger in the shadows, she hurried to her door. After swiping her key card through the lock to her suite, Trish slipped inside and locked the door behind her.

More shadows danced in the corners of her room, and the wind rattled the balcony doors. Not wanting to remain in the spooky confines of her suite and anxious to find Deb, she donned a heavier jacket and grabbed the flashlight she'd packed in her luggage. She was ready to hit the trail again.

The prospect of the dark, lonely mountain paths terrified her, but she was even more afraid of not finding Debra...before it was too late.

Chapter Six

O'Neill couldn't take his eyes off Erin as she crossed the porch toward Victoria Westbrook at the buffet table. He tried to analyze the powerful connection he felt, unlike anything he'd ever experienced. But no matter how he looked at it, the attraction didn't make sense, especially considering he'd spent only a few hours in her company.

But what hours they had been.

She had surprised him again today, this time with her strange reaction on the trail after lunch. Either she was the world's greatest actress or something had scared the living daylights out of her. When she'd leapt to her feet, blue-green eyes wide with alarm, cheeks that reminded him of ripe peaches flushed with deep color and her breath coming in short gasps, she looked as if she'd seen a ghost.

And then she'd announced her crazy desire to keep searching, alone and in the dark, for Debra Devlin. Erin was either the bravest woman he'd ever known or a fool, but he couldn't accept the latter possibility. There was definitely more to Erin Fairchild than met the eye, and O'Neill was determined to find out what she was hiding, if for no other reason than that his own secrets might be at stake.

Quinn Stevens had made his fortune in computer technology and had resources at his command that could unearth anyone's deepest secrets. As soon as O'Neill checked the search status at the command tent, he'd see about digging into Erin Fairchild's background.

Even now, some sixth sense warned O'Neill not to leave her, but he shook the feeling off. She was perfectly safe among the guests and staff.

But what if she's come to cause trouble, an inner voice taunted.

Then he'd return to her as quickly as possible, just in case.

O'Neill left the porch and dropped the rucksack in the kitchen with Henry, the sous-chef. He strode through the empty dining room, out the glass doors and across the terrace. When he reached the command tent, he was surprised to find Metcalf still on duty.

"Don't you ever sleep?" he asked.

The sheriff jerked his thumb toward a roll-away bed folded in the corner. "Ms. Conover brought that earlier, and I grabbed a few winks this afternoon."

Janine Conover, the resort's assistant manager, had taken good care of the rescue squad in O'Neill's absence. "Anything turn up on the Devlin woman?"

"Nothing. It's as if she's disappeared into thin air."

"Will the search teams head out again tonight?" He'd promised Erin he'd ask them to search the path again where the cell phone had been found, but he was reluctant to explain the reason to Metcalf, a no-nonsense guy who would probably scoff at the woman's baseless entreaty. The sheriff's next words saved O'Neill from requests or explanations.

"No one's going out tonight. Too dangerous. There's a massive cold front on our doorstep. In a couple of hours, this area will be socked in with rain, sleet, even snow at these higher elevations."

"That doesn't bode well for Ms. Devlin, if she's out there."

Metcalf shook his head. "Exposure, hypothermia. If the woman's survived this long, it'll be a miracle. She won't make it through tonight."

"So you've suspended the search?"

"Only temporarily. After this front has moved through, we'll be calling additional searches for recovery, rather than rescue."

In other words, they'd be looking for a body, O'Neill thought with a shudder. "Is the front moving fast?"

Metcalf set his lips in a grim line. "It's

predicted to stall over the mountains. It could be twenty-four hours before the weather clears again."

"Damn."

Pity for the woman, who, if alive, was alone, injured and freezing to death in the wilderness, rolled through O'Neill.

He thought back to the day she had disappeared. He'd given her maps of the trails and warned her against straying too far from the resort alone. She had laughed and claimed she had a keen sense of direction and her cell phone, and that she'd be fine. He'd explained that cell phone coverage was spotty at best along the parkway, but the day had been so glorious and she'd seemed so confident that he really hadn't worried about her.

Until too late.

If Debra Devlin had perished in the wilderness, her death would hang heavy on his conscience.

"The cadaver dogs will join the search," Metcalf said, confirming O'Neill's fears, "as soon as the weather clears."

"Is my staff looking out for you?"

"Everything's great," Metcalf said with irony. "Except for Ms. Devlin's disappearance, with all this fine food and fresh air, it's like being on vacation."

O'Neill left the tent and started across the lawn toward the resort. A flicker of light to the east caught his eye. At the entrance to the trail, he spotted Erin, her blond hair and shapely silhouette unmistakable, even in the darkness with her bundled in a heavy jacket. As he watched, she disappeared among the rhododendrons.

Had the woman lost her mind, tackling that trail alone at night? Metcalf's weather forecast rang in his ears and O'Neill's sense of urgency heightened.

"Erin!" he shouted, but the freshening wind caught his cry and blew it back at him.

Determined not to lose another guest to the elements, especially Erin, who'd pierced his defenses and touched his heart, he sprinted to his rooms to grab rain gear and a handheld searchlight before going after her.

STEPPING OUT of the underbrush onto the barren ridge, Trish turned off her flashlight. The ambient light of the full moon provided all the illumination she required. She hurried along the level path that ran atop the ridge, anxious to place herself as far from Endless Sky as possible before O'Neill realized she was gone. She didn't want him following and forcing her to return. She'd come to these mountains to find Debra, and she wouldn't allow O'Neill to dissuade her.

When she had first stepped onto the open ridge, her fear of high places had paralyzed her. In every direction, the world fell away beneath her feet, and the endless folds of mountains loomed in the darkness like the backs of giant beasts. From behind, a strong, cold wind, like a willing conspirator, pressed her forward.

Memories of her sister—flashes from their childhood and teens, and from recent lunches and shopping sprees—helped her overcome her paralysis. She wrapped the pleasant thoughts around her like a shield against her fear of heights and her terror at being alone in the wilderness and wished for O'Neill's reassuring presence. By hiking with him, although she hadn't felt completely safe, at least she hadn't been totally alone. Despite his air of aloofness mixed with a subtle hint of danger, she'd felt a closeness to the man she couldn't explain. But the attractive resident manager couldn't know she'd heard Deb's voice, giving her hope that her sister was still alive. Probably wouldn't believe Trish, even if she told him, and would only block her search.

She'd never met a man who affected her as O'Neill had. When she was with him, she often felt as she had when she crested the highest peak of the monster roller coaster at Busch Gardens and plunged downward, her heart in her throat, half scared, half exhilarated. Under different circumstances, she would have enjoyed getting to know O'Neill better, even though, according to Victoria, such an endeavor would be an exercise in futility. Even if the inscrutable resident manager were to show an interest in her, she was at Endless Sky under false pretenses and a fake name, inauspicious circumstances for any relationship.

Relationship, she thought with a bitter laugh. *Fat chance.* She had nothing in common with the man, knew nothing about him except that he spent half the year in the mountains, half in the Caribbean, and that he kept his distance from women. Worry over Deb had made her crazy, or she wouldn't be having such fantasies. The only good that came from speculating about O'Neill was the warmth such thoughts sent spiraling through her, protection against the bitter cold and icy wind.

After what seemed a lifetime on the trail atop the ridge, Trish followed the path as it dipped into the mottled shadows of the forest of dead balsam firs, their gray branches twisting like tortured wraiths in the strengthening wind. Eerie in the daytime, the dead trees were even more forbidding by night. Trish hurried through them and their skeletal branches seemed to grasp at her, snagging her clothing as she passed. Her heart thundered in her throat, but not loud enough to cover the maniacal howl of the growing gale.

She descended into the deciduous forest where the thick canopy of leaves thrashed as if in agony above her head and blocked the moonlight. The bobbing circle from her flashlight revealed only a few feet of path in front of her. The pitch-black night, filled with strange noises and the wailing wind, closed around her.

Terror clawed at her and only the thought of Deb, also alone in the darkness, kept her going.

Do not fear. You do not walk alone.

The ancient voice that she'd heard last night in her suite and again that afternoon froze her steps. Her chest tight with fear, she flicked the beam of her flashlight around her.

You cannot see me. I am a spirit. And I am a friend. Do not be afraid.

"That's easy for you to say." Trish spoke

through chattering teeth, sounding braver than she felt.

Not all can hear me. You have the gift.

Lucky me, she thought with irony. The telepathic ability she'd developed in childhood to communicate with Debra must have somehow facilitated her contact with whomever…whatever was speaking to her.

"Who are you?"

I have been sent to watch over you.

Trish shivered in the cold, struggled for breath, and wondered if she'd lost her mind. "A guardian angel?"

A spirit. You must hurry. Your sister waits.

"Debra is here?"

Follow the path on which your feet are set. You will find her.

Trish moved forward. The gale shrieked around her. Icy darts of sleet pricked her cheeks and freezing air burned her lungs. Bushes and shrubs contorted, tormented by the violent wind, and branches slapped her face as she passed. Several times, without the support of the walking stick, her feet slipped out from under her, and she stumbled and pitched forward down the steep incline. Each time, she struggled to her feet, brushed forest debris from her clothes and hair, and pushed onward.

As she walked, she prayed harder than she had ever prayed in her life for courage and the strength to keep going. She bargained with God, promising to abandon her wicked ways if He'd just let her find Deb. But, like a sinking ship with no freight to throw overboard, she could think of few bad habits to forfeit: occasional overindulgence in chocolate, an orderliness that drove her friends crazy and a tendency to break the speed limit on her way to work. She owed her lack of sins more to a boring life than a good one. In desperation, she bartered her own life in exchange for her sister's.

By the time she'd reached the bottom of the ravine, crossed the creek and headed up the steep slope where she and O'Neill had stopped for lunch, her hair and clothes were soaked from wind-driven rain and plastered against her skin. Her teeth chattered violently from cold and fear. Only by continuing to move did she keep from freezing to death. Even her spirit guide, she noted with irony, had had sense enough to get in out of the weather. Either that, or, if he was still around, he'd gone completely silent.

Trish?

Deb's voice, reverberating in her mind, provided the impetus Trish needed for the long struggle to the top of the next ridge. There, the trees gave way to another barren expanse. In the darkness, only the beam from her flashlight prevented her from stumbling off the path and over the edge of a rock face that fell away into nothingness at her feet.

Deb? Are you here?

I'm here, Trish. I knew you'd come.

O'NEILL TOOK THE STEPS to his bedroom three at a time, yanked a hooded poncho from his closet and grabbed the heavy searchlight from its charger beside the bed. Sleet pattered against the windowpanes and prompted him to return to the closet for a second poncho. Once he caught up with Erin Fairchild, she'd need protection from the elements.

And from him.

He'd gladly wring her pretty neck for putting herself in danger. He couldn't understand Erin's obsession with finding the missing reporter, a woman she didn't even know. Or maybe her reckless quest had nothing to do Debra Devlin. Maybe Erin Fairchild had a death wish. Just because his clients were wealthy didn't mean they were logical. Or even sane. He had to be crazy himself to go after Erin in this weather. But the rescue squads were already exhausted. Better that he nip Erin's nocturnal excursion in the bud and save them an additional search.

He was already far behind her. A supposedly urgent summons from the Averys had slowed him down. By the time he'd contacted Janine to deal with their complaint that had turned out to be about the quality of their dinner, he'd lost precious time. In his frustration, he swore, louder than the wind that buffeted the house. He'd caught a glimpse of Erin's fair hair and pale hands in the moonlight before she disappeared into the underbrush. She hadn't worn a hat or gloves, much less rain gear. She'd be soaked and freezing if he didn't bring her back quickly.

As he hurried through the house, he debated telling Metcalf where he was going and decided against it. The sooner O'Neill caught up with Erin and forced her to return, the less exposure she'd suffer.

Why not send the rescue squad after her? the rational part of his brain demanded.

The question almost stopped him short, pointing out a reality he hadn't faced until now. Besides feeling a personal responsibility, he cared what happened to her. With her sunny smile, flashing eyes and unpredictable personality, Erin was inching her way into his heart. O'Neill, who'd always inclined toward being a loner, had purposely chosen his solitary existence after friends had disappointed him and Alicia betrayed him. Why had he allowed Erin to breach his well-manned defenses?

He shoved the question away and concentrated on the task at hand. Introspection would only slow him down. The screen door of his cottage slammed behind him, and he raced up the hill and across the lawn toward the path through the rhododendrons. He didn't need the searchlight yet. The encroaching clouds hadn't reached the moon. And he knew this trail so well that he could have followed it even in the dark.

But Erin didn't know the trail at all, and she was terrified of heights. She might panic, suffer vertigo and fall. And from every point on the ridge path, it was a long, brutal way down. He hastened his steps, kicking pebbles from the path as he hurried along the top of the ridge. Even with her twenty-minute lead, surely he'd catch up with her soon.

He scanned the terrain ahead as he ran, but saw no sign of Erin's silhouette. He hoped that meant she'd reached the downward trail safely. If she had fallen, he wouldn't be able to hear her cry for help above the screaming wind.

Plunging into the stand of dead balsams, he switched on his searchlight. Its powerful beam lit the trail ahead, but it was empty. Wind-driven sleet stung his face, but O'Neill pressed on, wondering how Erin could have moved so fast and praying that she hadn't disappeared into thin air like Debra Devlin.

He reached the deciduous forest and played the searchlight down the length of the path to the creek. No sign of Erin. Had she lost her way and taken another trail by mistake?

At that instant, the wind dropped and the forest grew still. In the lull, a scream pierced the silence.

"Erin," he yelled, "is that you?"

O'Neill turned in a circle and tried to identify the direction of the cry, but the wind had picked up again, drowning all other sounds.

Forcing himself to relax and think, O'Neill assessed his options. Should he double back and see if Erin had missed this trail or continue in the direction that she had wanted to take earlier today?

Through the wind-thrashed leaves above, a faint but steady light glimmered at the top of the next ridge. It wasn't moving. Had Erin dropped her flashlight?

The possibility of her lying hurt on the path propelled him down the incline in a headlong rush. Ignoring the burning in his lungs and the scream of his calves, he leaped over the creek and started up the opposite ridge. As he climbed higher, he again made out the circular glow of a flashlight, lying on the path, but Erin was nowhere to be seen. Recalling the trail's terrain, he realized with a sinking feeling in the pit of his stomach that the light lay by an overlook above a sheer rock face that dropped a thousand feet straight down.

Had the scream been Erin, falling?

The thought provided an extra rush of adrenaline, and he pushed uphill until he stood on the path beside the flashlight. Sweeping the broad beam of his searchlight in every direction, he caught no sign of Erin on or near the path.

With dread pounding in his veins, he stepped to the edge of the overlook and trained the light downward. A strong blast of wind at his back threatened to send him over the edge. He windmilled his arms, regained his balance and stepped back from the precipice.

Erin was a petite woman, only slightly over half his weight. Had the violent wind swept her off the cliff to the trees a thousand feet beneath the overlook? He braced for a glimmer of blond hair and pale face far below, but nothing broke the dark blanket of rock and forest that lay at the foot of the cliff.

Relieved, he moved from the edge and played his light farther up the path.

Where the hell was she?

The wind died briefly again, and an eerie moan filled the silence. O'Neill moved closer to the overlook's rim and leaned forward.

Several yards below on a rocky outcrop

barely inches from a sheer drop down the steep side, pale blond hair flashed against the dark, wet stones.

Erin had fallen from the overlook.

Chapter Seven

O'Neill scanned the vertical face of the cliff directly below him and cursed his failure to bring a rope. Searching frantically for a way to reach Erin, he finally spotted a break in the shrubs where a narrow path led downward. He lunged down the steep trail. Loose rocks and pebbles scattered beneath his feet, and several times he had to grab a branch that overhung the trail to keep from pitching headfirst down the mountainside.

The path ended abruptly on a narrow rock ledge that offered a dizzying drop to the forest a thousand feet below. O'Neill stepped onto the shelf that projected outward only a few feet and swept the underside of the ledge with his searchlight.

Erin's aqua eyes stared at him from beneath the wide overhang. She huddled over another person, prone and unconscious. O'Neill instantly recognized the woman's dark hair and colorful clothing.

Miracle of all miracles, Erin had found Debra Devlin.

"Is she alive?" he shouted above the roar of wind.

Erin nodded and shouted back. "The overhang sheltered her from rain and wind. That's the only thing that saved her. But she's freezing, and her pulse is slow."

Fanning his light, O'Neill inspected the cliff above them, but the only way out was the way he'd come in, a trail with an almost vertical incline. To add to the problem, thick wet flakes of snow had begun to fall.

"She needs a doctor," Erin insisted.

O'Neill frowned. "We shouldn't move her. She could have broken bones, internal injuries—"

"She'll die if we don't get her out of this cold. We have to chance it."

Erin was right, and they had no time to waste while they considered alternatives.

"I'll carry her," he said. "You take the light and come behind, in case I need a boost."

O'Neill maneuvered past Erin on the ledge and knelt beside the unconscious reporter. Her shorts and lightweight shirt provided no protection against the wind and snow. He handed Erin the searchlight and shrugged out of his jacket beneath his poncho. He tugged it and his extra poncho over Debra. The garments would provide only minimal warmth, but at least they would keep her dry. He lifted her in his arms, slung her over his shoulders in a fireman's carry and staggered dangerously close to the edge of the narrow ledge. Erin grabbed him and restored his balance. Shifting his deathly quiet load, he sidled along the rock shelf and started up the trail. Erin followed, playing the light ahead of him.

Their progress was agonizingly slow. Every step had to be calculated. One slip would send all three backward down the path and over the cliff. His muscles strained under the unaccustomed weight and his lungs protested. At one point, only the firm push of Erin's hands against his buttocks enabled him to keep moving upward.

They reached the overlook at the top of the trail, but he didn't stop to rest. Snow was accumulating fast and covering the path. With a sinking heart, he realized they would never make it back to the resort before becoming lost in the blizzard that was increasing in ferocity by the second.

While he paused and struggled for breath, Erin flicked the searchlight around them. Her eyes widened as the peril of their situation struck her. "Snow's covered the path. We can't see the way."

"Don't worry." With reluctance, but no other choice, he decided to break his promise and reveal a secret he'd sworn to keep. Lives were on the line. "There's shelter nearby where we can wait out the storm."

"But Debra needs medical care."

"We can't get help until the weather

breaks. For now, shelter and warmth are her best hope."

Employing his detailed knowledge of the surrounding terrain, O'Neill headed downhill toward the creek. There, instead of heading up the next ridge toward Endless Sky, he followed the creek downstream. Erin stayed close behind, shining the light ahead of them.

"How far?" she called above the wind that blasted snow at them in a blinding curtain.

"Not far," he lied and prayed they'd reach their destination before the swiftly falling snow obliterated the landmarks he needed to find his way.

Almost half an hour later, he topped a short rise and pointed ahead. "We're here."

TRISH'S FEET were blocks of ice, and her aching leg muscles could barely lift them. Even holding the searchlight seemed too much effort. She had never been so tired. The prospect of giving up, lying down in the soft snow and dropping off to sleep lured her. But Deb needed her, so she had to keep going. Just when she'd exhausted her last reserves of energy, O'Neill announced that they'd arrived at their destination.

Trish peered through the blowing snow and gasped in surprise. When O'Neill had stated shelter was nearby, she'd expected a rustic hunting cabin with primitive facilities. From what little she could glimpse through the thick curtain of snowflakes, the house before her was a miniature version of Endless Sky. Yellow light glowed from the twin front windows like the eyes of a night predator, lying waiting in the darkness. Not exactly the most attractive welcome, but she'd take refuge in a bear's den if it meant getting Deb out of the cold.

"Does someone live here?" she asked.

"No, the lights are on a timer," O'Neill explained, wheezing under the weight of a still-unconscious Debra. "There's a combination lock on the front door." He rattled off the code. "Open it for us."

Trish plowed ahead through the swirling white flakes, dragged her weary feet up the porch steps drifted with snow and punched in the numbers on the lock at the front entrance. When she opened the door, glorious warmth engulfed her. O'Neill followed close on her heels and carried Debra inside.

Trish barely noted the well-furnished living room as she trailed O'Neill into an adjoining bedroom.

"Pull back the covers," he ordered.

Trish quickly complied, and he laid Debra with extraordinary gentleness onto the soft, clean sheets of the king-size bed.

"I'll let you get her out of her wet clothes," he said, "while I bump up the thermostat. There's an electric blanket on the bed. It'll help bring her core temperature up."

O'Neill left the room. Sick with worry over Deb, who was too quiet, too cold, too pale, Trish stripped off the poncho that had been only partially effective in keeping her sister dry. She removed O'Neill's jacket and Deb's other clothing and noted with dismay the bruises on her sister's body and the unnatural angle of her left ankle.

Oh, Deb, what's happened to you?

But her sister had slipped so deeply into unconsciousness that she hadn't been able to respond, not even telepathically, since Trish had found her.

Trish tugged the covers to her sister's chin and turned the setting of the electric blanket on high. She bundled Deb's soggy clothes, stripped off her own wet jacket and tossed the garments onto the tile floor of the adjoining bathroom. Returning to the bedside, she pulled a chair close and sat.

O'Neill appeared at her elbow and grasped her shoulder. "Your turn," he said.

"What?"

"Your clothes and shoes are soaked." He handed her a navy blue velour robe and pointed to the bathroom. "We can't take care of her if we're sick ourselves. Get out of those wet clothes."

His intense midnight-blue eyes and his dark hair, snarled by the wind and damp with snow, gave a wildness to his appearance. For a fleeting instant, Trish feared being alone, God only knew where, with a stranger. Then she recalled his gentleness with Debra and the fact that he'd risked his life in a blizzard to come after her and to rescue her sister. Her fear eased and gratitude surged in its place.

"I don't know how to thank you," she said, recognizing that the truth about her identity would be a start, but she was too exhausted to deal with that complication right now.

His lips quirked in a crooked smile that softened the harsh planes of his face and made him look less dangerous. "Thank me by getting dry, so I don't have two sick females on my hands."

O'Neill was right, but she was reluctant to leave her sister, even for a few minutes. Trish glanced at Deb. "I think her ankle's broken."

He knotted his face in a frown. "She must have fallen from the overlook."

"And crawled under the overhang?"

He nodded. "It sheltered her from the elements, but it also prevented the rescue teams from locating her. How did you find her?"

"I heard her calling. She must have regained consciousness for a few minutes," Trish lied. Now that Deb had been found, Trish could reveal her true identity, but not yet. She was too tired for explanations. And he'd never understand her telepathic communication with her sister, so she wouldn't divulge how their psychic connection had led her to Deb.

O'Neill stepped into the bathroom and returned with a digital thermometer. Pushing Deb's thick hair aside, he gently inserted the instrument into her ear. When the thermometer beeped, he removed it and checked the readout. "A few degrees below normal, but the electric blanket should help. Did you notice any injuries besides her ankle?"

Trish shook her head. "Just lots of horrible bruises. But if she's hurt internally…" Her voice broke and tears welled in her eyes.

She'd found Deb, but her sister literally wasn't out of the woods.

O'Neill reached for Trish and pulled her against him. Through their wet clothes, the reassuring heat of his body enveloped her. Wrapped in his arms, she felt safe and was almost persuaded that Deb would be all right. With a start, she realized she wanted more than his embrace. Her lips tingled at the thought of kissing his, and she shivered as much from the unexpected desire that had ambushed her as from the cold.

O'Neill squeezed Trish in a fierce hug and, to her disappointment, released her. "Your clothes are soaked. Change into this dry robe. I'll fix something hot to drink."

He left the room and, after a quick check to assure herself that Deb was breathing naturally and her pulse was strong, Trish went into the bathroom. A glance in the mirrored expanse above the lavatory had her stepping back in alarm, until she realized the wild-eyed, desperate woman with tangled hair who confronted her was her own image.

Her gaze traveled from the beveled mirror to the cream-colored Italian marble of the floor and shower to the gold-plated fixtures. The decor, expensive yet understated and tasteful, made her wonder if the house was a private annex of Endless Sky.

And if this was an annex, there had to be an access road, a way for emergency vehicles to reach them.

Trish swiftly stripped her wet clothing, tugged off her soaked shoes and socks, and pulled on the soft robe. Obviously meant for a man, the velour garment almost touched the floor. She tied the robe tightly at the waist and rolled up the sleeves to free her hands.

Giddy at the prospect of imminent rescue, she hurried out of the bathroom, checked once more on Deb, who was breathing steadily but showed no sign of regaining consciousness, and went in search of O'Neill.

In her concern for Deb, she'd hardly noticed the living room earlier, but now she was struck by the casual comfort of the space with its high beamed ceiling, overstuffed furniture in a woodsy burgundy-and-green plaid, and a huge stone fireplace where O'Neill had lit a cheerful blaze.

Grateful for the growing warmth that chased the bone-deep chill from her body, she crossed the room and entered the kitchen.

O'Neill, his dark hair standing in spikes from an apparent toweling, stood at the cooktop, stirring something in a saucepan. He wore dry jeans, snugly fitted and slung low on his hips, and a black crewneck sweater. His feet were bare. He looked up and smiled when she entered the room, and her stomach did a flip-flop at the intensity in his expression.

"I'm making spiced cider," he said. "It'll heat you up."

Desire blindsided her again. O'Neill's innate appeal, mixed with his efforts to save Deb, made him impossible to resist. With the warmth his smile had generated, if she were any hotter, she'd burst into flames. With a twinge of guilt, she shoved her longings aside. She shouldn't be thinking of her attraction to O'Neill, not while her sister lay in the next room in need of medical attention. She tore her gaze away and focused on an object on a nearby countertop.

"Is that a phone?" she asked.

"Yep." O'Neill reached into a cabinet beside the stove, removed spice containers and dropped cinnamon sticks, cloves and powdered ginger into the simmering cider.

"Does it work?"

He nodded.

"Shouldn't we call for help?"

"Wouldn't do any good." His calm attitude was irritating.

"Why not?"

"Because we're cut off by the blizzard."

"Surely there's some vehicle that can make it through this weather. A snowmobile?"

O'Neill shook his head. "Trails are too narrow, steep and rough."

"Even for the Hummer?" Trish asked in disbelief.

"Especially not the Hummer."

Her earlier sense of security was swiftly disintegrating. "Why not?"

"No roads."

"You're kidding?"

"We're literally in the middle of no-where, and the only way out is the trail we came in on. Or a helicopter, which can't fly in these conditions."

Trish sank onto a stool beside the island and looked around the large kitchen, beautifully decorated and fully equipped with every modern convenience. "There has to be a road. Otherwise, how did they build this place?"

O'Neill removed the pot from the stove and strained its contents into two handmade pottery mugs. He handed one to Trish and leaned beside her, his hips against the island, one foot propped on the cabinet below. The easy calm of his attitude irritated her. "This is Quinn Stevens's personal hideaway. Besides him, only the workmen who built it and I know it's here."

She opened her mouth to speak, but he cut her off.

"As for how it was built, every tree removed to clear the land was carried out by helicopter. And all the building materials, furnishings and appliances were brought in the same way. So there was no need for roads. Stevens didn't want to destroy the environment by building a long access drive."

"But the electricity, phone lines—"

"Underground cables," he said, "buried at considerable expense, but if anyone can afford it, Stevens can. He has all the comforts of home here and no one to bother him."

She concentrated on her one ray of hope. "But there's room for a helicopter to land out there?"

He nodded. "As soon as the storm passes, we'll call for a chopper to airlift Ms. Devlin to the hospital in Asheville."

"Any idea how soon that will be?"

"Sometime tomorrow, if the weather report I heard was accurate."

"That long?" Her hopes sank. If Deb had internal injuries, the wait could be fatal.

O'Neill set down his mug and grasped her shoulders. "The phone's working. We'll call a trauma specialist at the hospital and ask his advice on how to care for our patient until we can medevac her."

Trish choked back a sob. She'd accomplished what she'd come for, to find her sister, but if Deb didn't get medical attention soon—

Before she realized what was happening, O'Neill had wrapped her in his arms. His hand smoothed her hair and his deep voice murmured in her ear. "Try not to worry. We'll take good care of her. I promise."

Frightened and exhausted, wrung out by the emotional and physical pressures of the past thirty-six hours, Trish yielded to the comfort of his embrace. With her cheek pressed against his broad chest, she could count the beats of his heart, a steady, reassuring rhythm. She slid her arms around his waist and reveled in his body heat that did more to chase the chill of worry over Deb from her bones than any hot cider ever could. He smelled of balsam-scented soap and leather and dryer-fresh clothes. She tilted her head and her gaze met his, dark and unwavering. "Why did you follow me?"

He cupped her face in his hands and his breath, fragrant with spices, fanned her face. "I knew the weather was turning bad. I couldn't leave you out in it."

"You could have sent the rescue squad."

"I thought I'd catch up with you faster than I did and make you turn back before the storm hit."

"So you were concerned for the resort's liability?" Even as she asked the pragmatic question, something far from practical flashed in his eyes.

"I was concerned for you."

"You barely know me." But she knew enough about O'Neill after his rescue of her and her sister to know that he was a good man, a man who had touched her heart.

"I intend to remedy that." He dropped his head and claimed her lips with his.

Caught by surprise, she yielded to his kiss. He tasted of spicy cider, and an excitement she'd never experienced shot through her veins.

Straddling the stool where she sat, he enveloped her with his body, his arms around her, his legs gripping her thighs. She laced her fingers through his thick hair and opened her lips to him. She tried to think of reasons to resist, but instead remembered his unselfishness, his compassion, and her resistance melted beneath his heat.

Time stood still, and nothing existed but the two of them, heartbeats and breathing synchronized. Their bodies melded as if forged in the heat of a white-hot flame, and all she wanted was closer, more. She felt as if she was where she truly belonged, as if she'd come home for the first time.

"Ah, Erin," he breathed.

The false name on his lips jerked her back to reality, and she broke from his embrace. Had she lost her mind? Her sister lay injured in the next room, and she was indulging in a passion party with a handsome stranger. What was she thinking?

A flush crept up her face. She knew exactly what she'd been thinking, wishing, hoping. And from the heated look in O'Neill's dark eyes, they'd been on the same wavelength.

He brushed her cheek with the back of his hand, and she resisted leaning into his touch.

"What's wrong?" he asked.

"Nothing."

Everything.

Deb was injured, and Trish wasn't who she'd claimed to be. Neither the time nor circumstances lent themselves to a relationship with O'Neill. The cold must have frozen her brain. "I'm just worried about Debra."

"You're right." He stepped away, but his reluctance to release her was clear. "I'll call the hospital."

She had to come clean about her identity and her relationship to Deb, as soon as—

Trish? Are you here or did I dream you?

Debra was conscious. Trish slid off the stool and grabbed her mug of cider.

"I'll see how she's doing." With her lips still burning from O'Neill's kiss, Trish hurried to the bedroom. She found her sister awake and propped on one elbow.

"Trish?" Deb's voice was cracked and rough, but whether from extended silence or days of screaming for help, Trish couldn't tell.

She rushed to Deb, put a steadying arm around her and thrust the mug into her hand. "Drink this. It'll warm you."

Deb took a few sips of the cider, then returned the cup to Trish with a shaky hand. "Where am I?"

"Quinn Stevens's private retreat. Is this what you were looking for when you fell?"

Deb grabbed Trish's forearm so hard her nails bit into the skin. "I didn't fall."

Deb must have hit her head, Trish thought, and was confused. "You *did* fall. I found you on the ledge beneath the overlook."

"I know. But I didn't fall," she insisted. "Someone pushed me."

Chapter Eight

"You were pushed?" Trish asked, stunned by the claim. "On purpose?"

Debra nodded. "I was standing at the overlook and heard something behind me. Before I could turn around, I felt two hands hit hard on my back. If that ledge hadn't been there to break my fall, I'd be dead now."

Not wanting to believe her, Trish looked into her sister's eyes, but she found no confusion, only anger and fear. "Do you know who pushed you?"

Deb shook her head and collapsed against the pillows. "That's why I hid under the ledge. I was afraid whoever shoved me off the overlook would come back to finish the job."

"That's a serious charge, Ms. Devlin." O'Neill stood in the doorway like a dark shadow, his expression unreadable.

Deb looked at O'Neill in surprise. "What's he doing here?" she asked Trish.

Trish suppressed a groan. She'd been so startled by Deb's story that she'd forgotten to warn her sister that she was at Endless Sky under a false name. "He carried you off the mountain. He saved your life."

O'Neill, one eyebrow cocked in speculation, glanced from Trish to Debra and back again. "You two know each other?"

Trish frowned. The moment of truth had arrived sooner than she'd planned.

Deb, unaware of her sister's charade, laughed, not the full strength of her usual chuckle, but a laugh nonetheless. "You could say we know each other. Trish is my sister."

"Trish?" O'Neill's eyes burned into Trish with the intensity of a laser. "Is Ms. Devlin delusional or is there something you'd like to tell me?"

A moan of pain slipped from Deb's lips.

"My ankle. It hurts like hell. And so does my head."

"Any painkillers here?" Trish asked.

O'Neill had already disappeared.

Debra gripped her arm. "I don't know who pushed me. Whoever it was snuck up from behind and shoved me before I could get a look at him—or her." She nodded toward the doorway where O'Neill had stood. "For all I know, it could have been him."

Trish shook her head. "Why would O'Neill risk his life to save you if he wanted you dead?"

Debra shrugged in confusion. "Why did anyone push me in the first place?"

Trish recalled the questions the FBI agents had asked about Deb's potential enemies and wondered if one had surfaced at Endless Sky. Or if, in her investigation, Deb had created a new adversary. "Did you meet all the guests at the hotel?"

"Every single one." Talking was obviously an effort. A thin white line etched Deb's lips, and her voice had a breathy quality. "I was digging into their back-grounds, especially the men in their thirties, trying to identify Quinn Stevens."

"Maybe someone was afraid you'd un-cover secrets best left buried. Especially since you're a reporter who might publish your findings."

Deb thought for a moment. "Or maybe I was too close to exposing Stevens's iden-tity and he, or someone he hired, stepped in to keep me quiet."

"Is he that ruthless?"

"Nobody knows." Deb closed her eyes. For a moment she appeared to have lost consciousness again, but she must have been gathering strength to speak. "There's no personal information available about the man. Not even a description."

"O'Neill knows him," Trish said.

"Can we trust O'Neill?" Deb looked frightened. "He owes his paycheck to Stevens. We don't know how deep his loy-alties run."

"What choice do we have?" Trish wanted to trust O'Neill, even though her sixth sense was sending her warnings she wished she could ignore. She didn't like to consider the alternative, that he had harmed her sister or hired himself out to do Stevens's dirty work. "I don't know where we are or how to get out of here. He says there're no roads."

"And you believe him?"

Trish hesitated. She believed O'Neill, but had her judgment been skewed by her strong attraction? Or had she been attracted to him because he seemed trustworthy? Her internal debate was making her head hurt.

O'Neill reappeared in the doorway with the handset from the phone in one hand and a bottle of Tylenol in the other. He offered the handset to Debra. "I have the trauma specialist on the line. He wants to talk to you."

Debra took the handset, and Trish watched and listened while her sister fielded the doctor's questions.

O'Neill retreated to the doorway, where he stood with one shoulder propped against the jamb and his arms folded across his chest, his neutral expression giving nothing away. Outside the blizzard raged, hammering the sturdy log house and howling in fury.

When Deb had answered all the doctor's questions, she passed the phone to Trish.

"Will you be caring for Ms. Devlin?" the doctor asked.

"Yes, for now."

"Give her Tylenol for pain. Rehydrate her, as much warm liquid as she can take. No solid food. And keep her quiet."

"What about her ankle?"

"If you know first aid, you can put it in a splint. Otherwise, it's best to leave it. Let me speak with O'Neill, please."

Trish returned the handset to O'Neill.

He stepped into the room and took the phone. "O'Neill here." He listened for a moment. "Thanks for your help, Doctor. Call me at this number when the medevac chopper is cleared to fly."

He turned off the handset and looked to Deb. "What's the diagnosis?"

Deb, exhausted by her conversation with the doctor, lay back on the pillows. "Inconclusive until he can examine me."

"Do you know how to apply a splint?" Trish asked O'Neill.

He shook his head. "Never took a first-aid course. Sorry."

Trish returned her attention to Deb. "Guess we'll have to leave your ankle to the doctor."

Deb's face was pinched with pain. "Just give me something to make it and my head stop throbbing."

Trish hurried into the bathroom, filled a glass with water and returned. She handed Deb two extra-strength Tylenol and the glass. Deb placed the capsules in her mouth, washed them down and settled back against the pillows once more.

Trish left the glass and the mug of cider by the bed. "You should drink all of that and then rest. I'll be close by. Just call if you need me."

Trish started for the door.

Thanks, sis. I knew you'd come for me.

I love you, Debster. Just hang on until we can get you out of here.

O'Neill followed and closed the door behind him.

THE CLOCK on the mantel chimed midnight. O'Neill laid another log on the fire and settled into the deep chair across from Erin.

No, not Erin Fairchild. Trish Devlin, he reminded himself.

That bit of information and the fact that she was Debra's sister cleared up one mystery. Her unusual concern for the missing reporter now made sense, although how she'd managed to locate her sister when the rescue teams had failed could only be chalked up to amazing luck.

Unless there was more the secretive Trish wasn't telling him.

Beneath half-closed eyelids, he watched her by the flickering light from the fireplace. She was a study in contradictions. She'd been strong enough to brave the wilderness and the elements to search for her sister, but sitting there now, staring at the fire, bare feet curled beneath her and the sleeves of the too-big robe turned back from her slender hands, she looked fragile and vulnerable.

And scared.

"Do you believe Debra?" he asked.

"About what?" Her blue-green eyes seemed deep enough to drown in.

"That someone pushed her."

Her delicate nostrils flared. "Deb doesn't lie."

"Unlike her sister?"

"Touché." A flush stained her high cheekbones.

"Why the masquerade?"

"The Tampa FBI agents made me suspicious—and extra cautious—with questions about Deb's enemies. I decided I could learn more about what had happened to her if no one knew we were related."

He grudgingly conceded the logic of her explanation. "So, if you're not a distant relative of the Fairchild family, who are you?"

"Just a middle-school teacher from Tampa."

"Married?"

"No! I mean, I wouldn't have…" She appeared to grope for words, and her flush deepened.

"Kissed me?" He exerted all his self-control to keep himself from going to her and kissing her again.

She shook her head. "Not if I was married."

"Or engaged?"

She shook her head again.

"Regrets?"

She pursed her pretty lips. "Time will tell. Right now, I'm more worried about Deb."

As much as he wanted to kiss her again, he forced his attention to the dilemma of the woman in the next room. Leaning forward in his chair, he clasped his hands between his knees. "We have a problem."

Her remarkable eyes widened, and her irises reflected the flames from the fireplace. The fire shot streaks of gold through her pale blond hair, tousled from the wind. She looked sexy and vulnerable, a knockout combination. "Deb's injuries?"

"That, too," he admitted, tamping down his desire. "But I was thinking more about a potential murderer. If whoever pushed your sister learns she's alive, he—or she— might come after Debra again."

Trish wrinkled the smooth skin of her forehead in a frown. "I've been so worried about Deb's injuries, I hadn't thought of that. Can we keep her rescue a secret until we discover her attacker?"

O'Neill shook his head. "We can't allow the rescue squads to continue the search. It's dangerous work and someone could get hurt."

"So what do we do?"

"Let me talk to Captain Metcalf and fill him in. Maybe he'll have a suggestion. I'll call him in the morning." The moan of the keening wind from the storm penetrated the thick log walls, and heavy snow beat against the windowpanes. "No one's out in this weather now."

Trish nodded and returned her gaze to the fire. Her shoulders slumped with fatigue. In minutes, her eyes had closed. If she was half as exhausted as he was, he marveled that she'd stayed awake this long.

Moving quietly, he checked on Debra, also asleep, then returned to the living room and sat across from Trish again. Allowing her past his defenses had been a mistake, but he couldn't help himself. Her courage and loyalty were impossible to ignore. From the first moment he'd seen her at the airport, she had roused deep feelings, emotions he'd believed sealed off forever. Watching her now, observing the gentle rise and fall of her breathing, the brush of dark lashes against flawless cheeks, her fragile facade that disguised a backbone of steel, he felt a rush of tenderness unlike anything he'd ever experienced for Alicia. Trish was insistent on taking care of herself, but he wanted to protect her, to shield her from unpleasantness and danger.

Most of all, he wanted to make love to her. He rose, went to her and scooped her up. She didn't waken but snuggled deeper into his embrace, and he marveled at how good she felt, as if she'd been made for his arms. He carried her into the other bedroom, tugged down the covers and laid her gently on the king-size bed.

Without waking, she curled on her side. O'Neill lay beside her and pulled the blankets over both of them. He slid his arm around her waist, and her crisp, clean scent enveloped him. Fitting his body to hers, he felt her warmth seep into him. In an instant, he dropped into the deep sleep of exhaustion.

A BLAST OF HOWLING WIND awakened Trish. She bolted upright and glanced around in confusion. She didn't recognize the room and couldn't remember how she'd gotten there. Dim recollections of lying tucked against a warm, hard body flitted at the edge of her consciousness. At first, she thought she'd been dreaming, but the indentation on the pillow beside hers and the faint scent of balsam confirmed that O'Neill had slept beside her. Not only that, but he had carried her to bed last night, as well.

The intimacy of lying curled against

O'Neill, even in her sleep, both thrilled and worried her. Events were moving too fast and, in her concern for Deb, Trish hadn't been thinking clearly. She had allowed emotions to overrule her reason. Her sharp intuition, as much a part of her as her psychic connection with her sister, told her that, although O'Neill obviously didn't intend to harm her or Deb, as evidenced by his selfless rescue, the man had deep secrets that he worked hard to hide. Under other circumstances, she would have kept her distance from O'Neill until she'd learned more about him, assessed his character and plumbed his motives, instead of making herself vulnerable to his charm.

And opening herself to his kiss.

Her pulse quickened at the memory until her pragmatic side took charge. She had to resist O'Neill and his magnetic appeal. Her first priority was taking care of Deb and finding out who'd tried to murder her sister. She swung her feet over the bed. Pale gray light seeped through the uncovered windows. Morning had arrived, but the storm hadn't abated. No helicopters could fly in this weather.

She pattered barefoot across the living room to check on Deb. Her sister slept soundly, and her color was good and her breathing even. Trish put her wrist on Deb's forehead and was relieved to find no hint of fever.

Trish returned to the room where she'd slept and headed for the adjoining bathroom. It was as elegant as the one off Deb's room. Stevens apparently didn't believe in roughing it. O'Neill had laid out fresh towels, a new toothbrush still in its package and toothpaste. Trish hurriedly washed her face, brushed her teeth and finger-combed her hair. She cinched the sash on her oversize robe, rerolled the sleeves, and went to reclaim her own clothes, even if they were still wet.

After she left the bathroom, the sound of a strange voice drew her to the kitchen. O'Neill stood at the cooktop, frying sausage. The tantalizing aroma reminded her she hadn't eaten since their picnic lunch yesterday, and her stomach growled with hunger. The voice she'd heard came from the radio, where an announcer was giving the local weather forecast.

"Good," O'Neill said when the report ended. "We can fly out of here later today."

"Fly?" The prospect of hovering high above the mountains in a tiny helicopter filled her with panic and she struggled to control her ragged breathing. As her fear of heights kicked in, her stomach revolted at the smell of food.

O'Neill's expression turned from jubilant to compassionate. "Afraid of flying?"

She nodded, still fighting for air.

He removed the sausages to a plate and slid diced potatoes and onions into the hot pan. "There's another alternative."

"What?"

"I called Metcalf this morning and told him we'd found Ms. Devlin. I also related her claim that she'd been pushed. He agrees we should keep her rescue secret for now."

Concern for Deb drove away her panic,

and her breathing slowly returned to normal. "How do we keep her location a secret without endangering the rescue squad in an unnecessary search?"

"The search is suspended until the storm passes. After that, Metcalf says there's no hurry, since, had we not found Deb, she wouldn't have survived this weather. Speed, while desirable, isn't as critical in a recovery effort, so Metcalf can claim that his squads and volunteers need another day to rest."

"But the media's all over this story," Trish said. "Won't they report that Deb's in the hospital?"

"Not if we admit her under an assumed name." His lips quirked in a wry smile. "You shouldn't have any trouble coming up with an alias, considering your own experience."

"I'm not normally deceptive," she protested.

He stared at her for a long moment before returning his attention to the hash browns. "I believe you. But we'll have to prolong your deception if we want to smoke out Ms. Devlin's assailant. And expand it."

"Expand it?"

"If we accompany your sister to the hospital, once we return to Endless Sky, we'd have a hard time explaining how we traveled to Asheville in a storm. Remaining here and hiking back to the resort when the weather clears makes better sense."

Trish didn't like to admit how much being alone with O'Neill appealed to her, in spite of her earlier protestations about remaining objective. "And how would we explain our absence?"

"If we return on foot, no one will know where we've been. I told Janine, my assistant, to take charge until further notice and not to disturb me. She thinks I'm at my house on the grounds."

Heat crept up Trish's face. "So we let everyone assume I've been there with you?"

"You have a problem with that?" His tone was light, breezy.

"I don't know if I can pull it off," she admitted, but didn't concede how the idea of spending time alone with O'Neill stirred her senses and warmed her heart. "I'm not exactly a femme fatale."

"You can do it to help your sister." His gaze burned into her. "And no one will have a problem believing I've fallen hard for you."

Was he implying that he had fallen for her? Her heart leaped at the possibility, but she shook her head. "Don't be so sure. Your imperviousness to women is a hot topic of conversation among female guests."

"Really?" He seemed genuinely surprised.

"Night before last, Victoria Westbrook was taking bets on who'd be the first to break through the barriers and kiss you."

"So you're the lucky winner." His smile was teasing and threatened to destroy her resolve to keep her distance.

"Why?"

"What?"

"Why me? You've made a reputation of avoiding involvement with female guests in the past." Her heart hammered and she held her breath, waiting for his answer.

He slid the hash browns onto a platter beside the sausages and set the pan back on the stove. Turning, he caught her in his stare, his midnight-blue eyes almost black. "You don't know me very well, do you?"

He'd hit the nail on the head, and Trish squirmed under his scrutiny. "That's the problem. I shouldn't have indulged in kissing a man I know so little about."

"What would you like to know?" He poured the bowl of eggs he'd been whisking into the heated pan.

"Anything would be a start."

"Then I'll begin with your last question. I kissed you because I couldn't think of anything I wanted more. And, until yesterday, I hadn't felt that way in over six years."

The flicker of pain in his eyes was impossible to miss. "What happened six years ago?"

He turned his attention to scrambling the eggs and ignored her question. When the eggs were fluffy, he transferred them to the serving platter, placed the pan in the sink, and sat at the island across from her. "You'd better eat while it's hot."

She filled her plate, but the knot of apprehension in her throat prevented her from swallowing. O'Neill helped himself to eggs, hash browns and sausage.

"Six years ago…" His voice was flat, devoid of all emotion. "I broke my engagement."

"Oh." He, not his fiancée, had broken his engagement. She wondered what had happened.

"Aren't you going to ask why?"

She shook her head. "I figure you'll tell me if you want me to know."

O'Neill met her gaze straight on and shook his head. "You're an unusual woman, Trish Devlin. Now eat your breakfast before it gets cold."

Her hunger overcame her nerves, and she dug into her eggs. For several long minutes, they ate with the muted strains of country music on the radio and the howl of the wind the only sounds in the room.

When O'Neill finished, he wiped his

mouth with a napkin and refilled his coffee mug.

"I discovered my fiancée was unfaithful," he said, picking up the conversation as if he'd never dropped it and revealing no more emotion than if he were discussing the weather. "Until then, I hadn't a clue that Alicia was an opportunist who wanted me only for my money and the perks of my lifestyle. She loved the good life I lead, not me."

Trish didn't need telepathy to sense the pain behind O'Neill's indifferent facade. "Her betrayal must have hurt."

"It taught me to guard my heart. Made me suspicious of women and their motives, especially the superficial types I meet at the resort." His detached demeanor warmed. "Until I met you."

"And now you know I'm deceitful, too." Thoughts of what might have been filled her with regret.

He shook his head. "You lied about your identity, but who you are is obvious."

"A middle-income schoolteacher who

doesn't belong among the rich and famous?" She flashed a self-deprecating grin.

He reached across the island and
threaded his fingers through hers. "A
woman who risked her life for her sister.
That's about as unselfish as it gets."

"Deb would have done the same for me."

He sighed. "I'm an only child. Guess
I've missed a lot, not having brothers or
sisters."

She squeezed his hand and grinned.
"Keep talking, O'Neill, and I'll know all
your secrets."

His expression closed, like a shutter
over a window. "We'd better check on
your sister."

Apparently, O'Neill, despite his revela-
tions about Alicia, still kept the secrets he
didn't want to share.

After breakfast, Trish took Deb orange
juice and hot tea and sat beside the bed to
make certain her sister drank them. She
could hear O'Neill talking on the phone in
the kitchen, and assumed he was directing
activities at the resort.

She must have dozed off in the comfortable bedroom chair, because the next thing she knew, O'Neill entered the room with a pile of neatly folded clothing, still warm from the dryer, including her sneakers. He was dressed in his jeans, sweater and hiking boots from the day before.

"I washed and dried our clothes," he said. "I'll sit with Debra if you want to take a shower and dress."

"Thanks." O'Neill was becoming harder to resist by the minute. Trish wondered if his thoughtfulness was an integral part of his character or merely an extension of his hotel hospitality.

"You'll be okay?" she asked Deb.

Her sister nodded. "I'm feeling stronger after a good night's rest. That must be a good sign."

Trish hurriedly showered, blew her hair dry and tugged on her clothes. When she returned to Deb, her sister motioned her to sit beside her.

"Did you find my computer?" Deb asked.

Trish shook her head and looked to O'Neill.

"The FBI took it," he said, "but the rest of your belongings are locked in a storage closet at my house."

"See if you can get my computer back," Deb said. "You'll want to review my notes on the guests and Stevens. The key to who pushed me may be in there somewhere." She gave Trish her password.

And be extra careful, she warned. *If my attacker learns you're my sister, he may come after you, too.*

Why?

I could have been attacked because I've learned something someone doesn't want revealed. If my attacker thinks I've shared the information with you, you're in danger, too. And I'm still not sure about O'Neill.

He could have left us to freeze to death on that ledge if he meant to harm us.

I can tell you like him, Trish. But the man's trouble.

You found reasons to be suspicious of him?

I found nothing about him. It's as if he doesn't exist.

"You should sleep now," Trish said, wondering what Deb's lack of background information on O'Neill meant.

But Deb had already closed her eyes.

Trish spent most of the day curled in the bedroom window seat, dividing her attention between the dwindling storm and her sister. O'Neill brought her lunch—a sandwich, cookies and hot tea—and returned to the kitchen and his phone calls. In the late afternoon, the clouds parted and brilliant sunlight glistened off the snow that covered the clearing around the house.

"The medevac chopper will be here soon." O'Neill came into the bedroom, carrying the robe Trish had worn the previous night, now freshly washed. He handed it to Deb. "Something to wear for your trip."

O'Neill left and Trish helped Debra into the robe. The thwack-thwack of helicopter rotors broke the silence. Outside, voices sounded and feet stamped on the terrace. Within seconds, two paramedics, a male and female, entered the room with a stretcher. They checked Deb's vital signs, stabilized her ankle with an inflatable cast and strapped her onto the gurney. Trish followed as they carried Deb toward the waiting chopper.

"I'll stay in touch by phone," Trish shouted above the noise of the waiting aircraft, "and I'll come to the hospital as soon as I can."

Don't worry about me. I'm in good hands. Take care of yourself.

Trish fought back tears. She'd come close to losing her sister forever, yet Deb's smile was brave, in spite of all that had happened. Trish hugged her sister, then stood aside as the paramedics loaded the stretcher into the chopper.

With O'Neill at her side, Trish waited on the snow-covered lawn and watched the helicopter ascend into the darkening sky, streaked with rose and coral from the rapidly setting sun. The chopper disappeared behind a ridge.

"Now it's our turn," Trish said.

O'Neill shook his head. "We're not going anywhere."

"But we have to get back to Endless Sky."

"It'll be dark in a few minutes," he said with exasperating reason. "And snow still covers the trails. We'll leave at first light in the morning."

Trish glanced around at the emptiness of the surrounding wilderness and at the huge house that loomed at her back. In her concern for Debra, she hadn't given a thought until now that she would have to spend another night with O'Neill.

Alone.

Chapter Nine

The last sounds of the helicopter, Trish's only contact with civilization, faded in the distance. Her sister was in good hands, and Trish had no fear for her own physical safety. But what about her heart? Deb hadn't trusted O'Neill. With Trish's finely honed instincts warning of too many secrets beneath his handsome but mysterious exterior, she wasn't ready to trust him completely, either, despite his help in rescuing her sister. The man and his motives were a puzzle she had yet to solve.

She also feared the feelings he engendered in her, turbulent emotions that could lead to heartache with a man she barely knew and, once she left Endless Sky, would never see again. Usually pragmatic and unflappable, she couldn't think straight where O'Neill was concerned. If she believed in superstitious nonsense, she'd wonder if he'd cast some sort of spell on her.

Unaware of her inner turmoil, O'Neill placed his arm around her shoulders and steered her toward the house. "You'll freeze if you stay out here much longer."

With the seductive heat of his touch flowing through the heavy fabric of her jacket, she yielded to his guidance. She was a big girl, she reminded herself, and could resist temptation. And she was suffering from stress, not O'Neill-spun magic. A sigh escaped her. She needed her head examined for having given in to his kiss. But what a kiss. If Deb hadn't been lying hurt in the next room, no telling where that encounter would have led.

Maybe where O'Neill was leading her now.

She applied the brakes to her crazy, runaway thoughts. Her own situation seemed inconsequential compared to Deb's problems. Trish tried to block the picture of her sister—pale, injured, strapped to a stretcher and flying high above the darkening mountain peaks—but she couldn't stop shivering at the image.

"Don't worry," O'Neill, seeming to read her mind, reassured her as they stomped snow from their feet and stepped inside. "The doctor promised to call as soon as he's examined Deb. She's going to be fine."

Trish nodded, but she couldn't stop worrying until she'd heard that optimistic diagnosis from the doctor himself. In the meantime, the best way to avoid a repeat of yesterday's dangerous kiss was to keep herself and O'Neill occupied with other things. She stripped off her jacket and hung it on a peg by the rear door.

O'Neill closed and locked the door against the cold and encroaching darkness. As he stood between her and the exit, pulling off his jacket, she felt a moment of panic. The man was enticingly masculine, mysterious and unpredictable. Her heart raced, and she felt suddenly afraid of what she was feeling. Operating solely on emotion would lead her into surefire trouble.

"Are there a pad and pencil somewhere that I can use?" she asked.

He cocked an eyebrow. "Why do you need paper and a pencil?"

She tore her gaze from the strong lines of his face, the intense dark blue of his eyes, and struggled to breathe. "I'm an inveterate list maker."

He went into the kitchen and began searching the drawers of the island. "I assume you're not talking grocery list, unless you know a store that makes impossible deliveries."

She followed, every nerve ending tingling with awareness of her isolation and the enigmatic man who shared it. "To find out who pushed Deb, we need a list of suspects and possible motives."

He stopped digging in a drawer long enough to fix her with a stare whose effect made her nervous. "You read too many mysteries."

She shrugged, unable to stop wondering what secrets O'Neill was hiding, and broke away from his gaze. "Books are all the training I have for a situation like this."

"Here we go." He pulled a legal pad and a ballpoint pen from the back of the drawer. "Will these do?"

"Perfect." She took them and perched on the stool beside the island.

"So who's at the top of your list?"

Trish didn't hesitate. "Quinn Stevens."

"Stevens isn't here."

"A man with that much money has a long reach." She wrote Stevens's name in block letters at the top of the page. "He owns the resort and he is, after all, the reason Deb came to Endless Sky."

O'Neill flicked on a set of pendant lights above the island and Trish noted that darkness had fallen and, according to the digital clock on the microwave, it was after seven.

"While you play Agatha Christie," O'Neill said, "I'll fix dinner."

"How come there's so much food here, if Stevens isn't?"

"Because part of my job is to keep this place well stocked, in case the boss decides to drop in at a moment's notice." He pulled a plate from the refrigerator. "Hope you like chicken. I took some out of the freezer to thaw earlier today."

"Chicken's fine." She wasn't hungry, but if cooking kept O'Neill occupied, the less likely he was to concentrate his attentions on her. "Does Stevens drop in often?"

"At least once a season, sometimes more." With the casual ease of someone accustomed to cooking, he washed the chicken breasts, placed them in a shallow dish and covered them with marinade from a bottle.

As much as she tried to concentrate on her list, Trish couldn't keep her eyes off the efficient movements of his well-shaped hands, the enticing angle of his strong jaw or the depth of blue in his eyes.

She forced herself back to the task at hand. "Where is Stevens when he isn't here?"

"Sometimes at his Saint Thomas resort. It's called Endless Sea. Then there's his house in Monterey, a condo in Miami, a ski lodge in Vail, a villa in the south of France...you get the picture."

"Does he have a family?"

O'Neill shook his head. "He's not married, if that's what you're asking. And none of his relatives, if he has them, has ever accompanied him here."

She shook her head. "That's sad."

He pulled his head from the lower cabinet he'd been searching and looked up in surprise. "Why sad? Most people would envy a man with so much real estate."

"All those homes and no one to share them with. He must be a very lonely man."

"He likes his solitude," O'Neill said. "That's why he built this house, away from everything."

"And everyone." She stared at the name on the page. "How well do you know your boss?"

O'Neill removed two large baking potatoes from a bin in the island and carried them to the sink. She couldn't tell whether his actions or his thoughts caused his brief hesitation. "As well as anyone else, I guess. Why?"

"Would he kill to guard his privacy?"

"That's a scary prospect." He scrubbed the potatoes beneath the kitchen faucet, pierced them with a fork, and placed them on the rack of the wall oven to bake.

"What happened to Deb is about as scary as it gets," Trish said, noting that he'd sidestepped her question.

O'Neill leaned his hips against the counter and folded his arms across his chest. "Agreed. But I don't see Stevens as a murderer."

Every nerve ending in her body tingled at the memory of being wrapped in those arms, but her brain still managed to function enough to carry on the conversation. "Why not?"

"He may be a loner, but basically he's a good guy. He treats his employees well and funds several large charitable foundations." O'Neill shrugged. "And with the power his money gives him, why would he resort to violence?"

"Because he's human? Mark Twain once said that, like the moon, we all have a dark side."

A smile softened the harsh angles of his face. "And you, Miss Schoolmarm, what's your dark side?"

She thought for a moment and remembered Deb, lying unconscious just inches from a fall to her death, and her own overwhelming rage when she'd learned her sister had been pushed. "I'm not sure, but whoever messed with my sister is going to feel the brunt of it, I swear."

Heat flared in his eyes, mesmerizing her. "Debra is lucky to have a sister like you."

The warmth from his gaze was drawing her into dangerous territory again. She focused instead on the name at the top of the pad that had her sixth sense on red alert. "My instincts tell me that somehow, even if only indirectly, Stevens is the key to what happened to Deb. If he's not the type to resort to violence, as you insist, does he have enemies who are less constrained?"

O'Neill closed his eyes for a moment, as if in thought, then opened them. "Chad Englewood had blood in his eye the other night when he complained about Stevens's cheating him in a real estate deal."

Trish added Chad's name to the list. "Who else?"

O'Neill went to the refrigerator, opened the freezer and surveyed its contents. "You like green beans?"

She couldn't help noticing that his shoulders were as broad and sturdy as the appliance. "Any vegetable is fine. Does Stevens have other enemies?"

O'Neill removed a bag from the freezer and placed it on the counter. He took a pot from the wrought-iron rack above the island, ran water into it and set it on the stove. "Stevens doesn't discuss his personal life with me."

"But you must have heard gossip? The man's a legend. He didn't become the Last

Man Standing without leaving a few bodies in his wake."

"You can't convict a man on gossip," O'Neill replied quickly and with irritating reason.

Trish wished she could explain to O'Neill about her instincts and her telepathic abilities, but past bad experiences with the reactions of others had made her closemouthed about her gifts. "Gossip might give us a clue to what's going on. I wish I'd paid more attention to business news."

"There's always Stevens's ex-partner, Blaine Carter." O'Neill's words came grudgingly. He dumped green beans into the boiling water in the saucepan, covered it and turned down the heat. "The press gives a lot of ink to that relationship, 'the dynamic duo of the computer world.'"

"If they made millions together, why would Carter have it in for Stevens?"

O'Neill straddled the stool across the island and clasped his hands on the granite countertop. "It's a long story."

"We're not going anywhere." And the

more she could keep O'Neill talking, the less she'd think about kissing him again, about being touched by those hands.

"Stevens and Carter were best buddies in high school," O'Neill said, "and still in their late teens when they started their dotcom company. The economy boomed and they became millionaires almost overnight. Stevens had a canny business sense and, several years later, foresaw the coming debacle among the dot-coms. He tried to convince Carter to sell the company, but Carter was greedy. He refused to believe the bubble was about to burst and wouldn't sell."

"So Carter lost everything?"

O'Neill nodded. "And he blamed Stevens."

"Why? Stevens warned him."

"Carter refused to sell his shares, but Stevens was adamant about dumping his half of the company. Carter, still thinking the dot-com would be his limitless cash cow, demanded to buy Stevens's interest and keep the entire company for himself."

"If you know so little about Stevens,"

she asked with suspicion, "how do you know this?"

"Unlike you, I do read the business news." He flashed a smile, but its warmth did nothing to chase the grim look from his eyes. Her instincts cued her that O'Neill knew more than he was telling.

"Did Stevens sell Carter his half?"

"Their contract gave each partner the right of first refusal in a buyout, so Stevens had no choice," O'Neill explained. "And this happened before the decline in dot-coms, so the company was still worth millions. It took almost every dollar Carter had to buy Stevens's half. Carter became sole owner, and Stevens walked away."

"And when the bubble burst, Carter went under?"

O'Neill nodded. "Lost everything. Stevens, on the other hand, was shrewd enough to catch the wave of the real estate boom. He invested his profit from the buyout in property and turned his millions into billions."

Trish doodled on her pad, drawing a box and a series of question marks around

Stevens's name. "But if Stevens warned Carter, why would Carter blame his ex-partner for his loss?"

"It takes a big man to admit his own mistakes," O'Neill said with a shake of his head. "Maybe it's easier for Carter to fault Stevens than to face his own greed and stupidity."

Trish tapped her pen against her chin. "Okay, for the sake of argument, let's say Carter does have it in for Stevens. How would harming Deb satisfy his revenge?"

O'Neill frowned. "I don't see how it would. The worst that would have happened to Stevens if Deb had died would have been some bad publicity for Endless Sky. Maybe a few guests would have canceled as a result, but, ultimately, Stevens would have emerged unscathed. I don't think Carter's our man."

"Which brings us back to Stevens."

"But why would he want to harm your sister?" O'Neill rose from the stool to place the chicken on the indoor grill. "It doesn't make sense."

Trish wasn't convinced of Stevens's innocence, not with her gut sounding alarm bells at the mere thought of him. "Deb's job is digging up facts. Maybe she dug up something about Stevens he didn't want revealed."

"She said she'd interviewed all the guests. She could have uncovered anyone's dirty secrets."

A glance at the clock revealed that not enough time had passed for Deb to have reached the hospital and undergone tests. As much as Trish wanted the phone to ring with the doctor's report, she resigned herself to waiting.

"So who goes on the list next?" she asked.

"Might as well start with the other guests in alphabetical order. That would be the Averys."

Trish shook her head. "They're too feeble to have hiked that trail and pushed Deb. And, from what Victoria told me, too poor to hire a hit man."

"Victoria Westbrook, Chad, Tiffany Slocum—"

"She's another reporter," Trish said.

"Maybe she was afraid Deb was going to scoop her on a story."

O'Neill frowned. "It would have to be a hell of a story to resort to murder in order to break it first. I don't think any of our guests, or Stevens, for that matter, are big enough news to kill for."

Trish counted on her fingers. "We've accounted for five of the eight suites. That leaves at least three guests I haven't met yet."

"There's Michael Redlin."

She hurriedly scribbled the name. "Tell me about him."

"He's from Nashville, a record producer. Made his fortune in country music."

"Is he here alone?"

O'Neill shook his head. "As manager, I'm supposed to be discreet."

"And also to protect your guests from harm," Trish reminded. "Who's here with him?"

"Tonya Devon."

"Wife of Dale Devon, the Grammy winner?"

O'Neill nodded. "But no one knows.

She's registered under an assumed name. Maybe Deb found out and—"

"Deb's a business reporter, not a gossip columnist," Trish said. "Besides, infidelity's one thing. Murder's another."

"Point taken." O'Neill turned the chicken on the grill and the succulent aroma filled the room. "That leaves only two other guests, Dan Beard and Austin Werner."

Trish added the names to her growing list. "What do you know about them?"

"Beard's from Kentucky. He owns racing stables."

"And Werner?"

"Apparently independently wealthy, but from what source, I haven't a clue," O'Neill admitted.

"What age is Werner?"

"Midthirties, as are Redlin and Beard."

Trish starred the men's names on her list. Looking for Stevens, Deb had concentrated her search on men in their thirties. O'Neill also fell into that age group. But Deb had said she'd found nothing about him.

"How come," Trish asked, "Deb couldn't find anything about you?"

O'Neill's expression turned guarded. "It wasn't for lack of trying. She grilled me with a ton of questions, but I never gave her enough to go on. Hard to find anything about a person when all you know is his last name."

"Why the secrecy?" Trish felt she was knocking on a door that she had no idea what was on the other side. A door that perhaps shouldn't be opened.

But O'Neill didn't hesitate in answering. "Maintaining a certain mystique is part of my job. Endless Sky is not only an exclusive resort, it's also famous for its eerie ambience. Remember the ghost stories I told you?"

Trish nodded. "And Ludie May added her share." She didn't tell him about hearing the voice of the ancient Cherokee. She had concluded that the phenomenon, a figment of her imagination, was the result of the power of suggestion and her hysteria over her missing sister.

"If everyone learns I'm just an ordinary guy from Chardon, Ohio," O'Neill said with an appealing grin, "my mystique goes down the drain. Better for business that I seem mysterious and dangerous."

If O'Neill was ordinary, she was the Queen of England. "What kind of ordinary guy are you?"

He lifted the chicken from the grill, dished out green beans and removed the potatoes from the convection oven. After filling two plates, he asked, "Want to eat here or in the dining room?"

"Here's fine."

Again he had avoided answering her question. He set two places with flatware and napkins, slid a plate across the island to her and sat down in front of his own. "Hope you're hungry."

Trish was too worried about Deb to have much appetite, but, for politeness's sake, took a bite of the chicken, which was tender and flavorful. "This is good."

"I aim to please."

"Then why didn't you answer my question?" The fact that O'Neill was pleasing in a very visceral sense made her skin flush.

His handsome face was the picture of innocence. "What question?"

"I asked what kind of ordinary guy you are."

"A boring one." He slathered butter on his baked potato. "I graduated high school and college, opened a business that eventually went under, then went to work for Stevens. That's about it."

While she couldn't fault his answer, it hadn't satisfied her curiosity. There were layers to O'Neill she hadn't peeled back yet, and she itched to know what lay beneath them. "Are your parents living?"

"They're retired."

"In Chardon?"

He shook his head. "They moved to Phoenix after Dad quit his job, and now they travel a lot. Free rooms at the resorts is one of my perks for working for Stevens, but they prefer St. Thomas over the mountains."

Trish wanted to ask about Alicia, his ex-fiancée, but his earlier attitude when speaking of her suggested she was a touchy subject. "You have any hobbies?" she asked instead.

"If this is twenty questions," he said with a searching look and a ghost of a smile, "do I get a turn next?"

"If I'm going to spend another night with a strange man," she shot back, "I should learn more about him first."

"I enjoyed sleeping with you." His gaze was heated and his eyes sparked with mischief. "Even if you do snore."

"I do not!"

"A very ladylike rumble, but a snore nonetheless."

"And I don't intend to sleep with you again," she insisted, fighting against her desire to do exactly that. "I was referring to staying under the same roof, that's all."

"No problem. There're two bedrooms." He polished off the last of his dinner, took his plate to the sink and flipped on the coffeemaker.

Trish, her face hot with embarrassment

and a touch of disappointment at his easy capitulation, handed him her plate.

"We can have coffee in the living room," O'Neill said, "in front of the fire."

"Fine, but you avoided my question again." Talking about O'Neill took the focus off her awkwardness. "The one about hobbies."

"Hobbies?" He thought for a moment. "I like to hike. The trails around here are one of the things I love about this job." He opened the freezer and removed a flat red box. "Cheesecake?"

"Sure. Nobody doesn't like Sara Lee." Trish was happy to inject a lighter note into the conversation, to shove aside the images of another night in O'Neill's arms. And with as much hiking as she'd done yesterday, she didn't have to worry about cheesecake calories.

O'Neill defrosted the dessert in the microwave, put their dessert plates, cups and saucers, and the coffee carafe on a tray, and motioned her toward the door to the living room.

Avoiding the sofa, Trish took a deep chair by the hearth. O'Neill set the tray on the coffee table, tossed extra logs on the fire and sat across from her.

Enveloped in the cozy, intimate atmosphere, Trish couldn't help contemplating what sharing coffee after dinner on a regular basis with O'Neill would be like, but she was too practical to let short-term attraction sidetrack her from her ultimate goal of a solid marriage, family and children. From everything she'd read and observed, the keys to a lasting relationship were honesty and commitment. She didn't know enough about O'Neill to discern if he was entirely honest—her instincts said otherwise—and commitment seemed a contradiction to his lone-wolf lifestyle.

In spite of his answers to her questions, she knew almost nothing about the man. His magnetic appeal drew her, but she sensed he held back, revealing as little of himself as possible. Maybe, as he'd hinted earlier, he'd been burned too deeply by Alicia to trust women.

Or maybe his secrets were more sinister?

Before she could follow that train of thought, the phone rang. O'Neill retrieved the handset from a nearby cradle and answered.

"I'll let you tell her," he said and handed Trish the phone.

"It's Deb," the familiar voice sounded on the other end of the line.

"Are you okay?" Trish asked.

"Except for a broken ankle. The doctor says I need a pin in it. But the MRI shows no other injuries."

"Will you need surgery?"

"Tomorrow morning, to insert the pin."

"I'll come see you no later than tomorrow afternoon. I promise."

"Don't worry. They're taking excellent care of me."

"I want to see that for myself."

"You be careful, sis. Whoever pushed me is still roaming free."

"I'll be careful. I promise. Love you, Debster."

"Love you, too. See you tomorrow."

With a sigh of relief, Trish clicked off the handset. Deb was going to be okay.

Without warning, in an inundating rush, all Trish's pent-up emotions of the past few days broke free. She hadn't cried when Deb had gone missing. She'd been too busy planning her own search. And once she'd found her sister, Trish had been too concerned over Deb's injuries to shed a tear. But now that Deb was in good hands with nothing worse than a broken ankle, a dam burst.

TRISH PUT DOWN the phone. O'Neill waited for a report, but she said nothing. She sat frozen, as if in a trance. A solitary silver tear slid down the perfect curve of her cheek, her sea-blue eyes filled with moisture and her shoulders trembled.

"Bad news?" he asked.

Trish shook her head. Her tears spilled over and ran down her face, and a sob racked her.

"What's wrong?" he insisted, alarmed at her distress.

"N...n...nothing," she uttered between her steadily increasing sobs.

Confused, but touched by her anguish, O'Neill left his chair and went to her. He picked her up, noting how delicate she seemed in his arms, then sat again and cradled her in his lap. Rocking her gently, he murmured against the silky texture of her hair. "That's a lot of crying over nothing."

She lifted her face and forced a smile through her tears. "She's going to be all right. Just a broken ankle."

"Isn't that good news?"

Trish sniffled and nodded. "But I've been so worried."

Now he understood. "Delayed reaction?"

She nodded again and gulped down a sob. "I can't stop."

He tightened his hold. "Shhh. Don't try. Let it all out."

"But I feel...so...foolish."

"You've been through hell. I'm surprised you've held up this long."

Trish Devlin was a remarkable woman who'd risked her life to save her sister, who hadn't given up, even when hardened and experienced members of the rescue squad had called it quits. Even while crying her eyes out, she maintained a certain dignity, an ethereal beauty. He cupped her face in his palms and wiped her tears with the pads of his thumbs.

He'd kissed her yesterday and the encounter had been like nothing he'd experienced before. It had left him longing for more. Propelled by the memory, he dipped his head and tasted the salty tears on her lips. He fully expected her to pull away, but instead, she opened her mouth to him and lifted her arms to encircle his neck. Heat surged through him like a cleansing fire and, in a moment of clarity, he wanted this woman more than he'd ever wanted anything in his life.

Against his chest, her heartbeat thudded, echoing his own, and her breath mingled with his. He threaded his fingers through her hair and pulled her closer, deepening the kiss.

She stiffened suddenly and drew back. "I shouldn't do this."

"You don't want to?" He released her, loath to force himself on her.

"Oh, I want to." Her voice was low, breathy, and he had to strain to hear. "Too much."

He traced the curve of her cheek with his index finger. Her skin was soft, smooth. "Then why stop?"

She climbed from his lap and moved closer to the fire. "Things are moving too fast. Especially when I'm not sure that they should be moving at all."

He struggled to concentrate, trying to understand her reasoning through the fog of his desire. "Why not? We're adults and neither of us has commitments to someone else."

She'd said she wasn't married or engaged, but she hadn't said there was no one else in her life. "You don't, do you?"

She shook her head and lifted her gaze past him, as if unable to meet his eyes. "But—"

Her eyes widened and she gasped in alarm.

Chapter Ten

O'Neill grabbed Trish by the shoulders. "What's wrong?"

She pointed to the window, filled now only with her own reflection, and blinked in surprise. "He's gone. Just disappeared into thin air."

O'Neill whipped around and stared where she'd pointed. "Who?"

"There was a man on the porch, looking in the French door." Someone *had* been there. She was sure of it. She couldn't stop shaking. Either O'Neill's tales of ghosts were true or she was losing her mind.

In three long strides, O'Neill crossed the room, threw open the door and stepped onto the porch. After searching its length, he came inside and locked the door. "Are you sure it wasn't a reflection? There're no tracks in the snow."

"I saw him as clearly as I'm seeing you now." Maybe she *was* losing it. Knees trembling, stomach fluttering, she sank into a chair. "He was tall with long, black hair, dark skin. And he was bare-chested."

"In this cold?" O'Neill shook his head in disbelief.

"He was dressed like an American Indian, all leather and beads. And paint on his face."

O'Neill stared with raised eyebrows.

"You think I'm crazy, don't you?"

He crossed to the glass-paned doors, drew heavy drapery over them and returned to her side. Contemplation, not disbelief, shone in his eyes. "If you are, you're not the only one."

"What are you saying?"

"Our Cherokee friend has been seen before."

"Here?" Trish didn't know whether to feel relieved or frightened.

"Not here. In the halls of Endless Sky."

"You've seen him?"

"No, but several guests and a few of the staff have reported an Indian in full battle dress hovering in the shadows." O'Neill frowned. "His appearance usually portends some dire event. The last time he was seen was right before one elderly guest suffered a fatal heart attack."

"Brought on by fright?" Trish's own heart was pounding like a jackhammer.

"The guest didn't see the apparition. Judd Raye, the custodian, encountered him in the basement while he was repairing a water heater."

"So this Cherokee is a harbinger of doom?"

O'Neill shrugged. "It could be coincidence."

Shivering despite the heat from the fireplace, Trish sank into a chair. "I hadn't seen him before, but I've heard his voice."

"He talks to you?" Now O'Neill did look skeptical, and she couldn't blame him.

"Either that or I've become suddenly schizophrenic with voices in my head."

"What did he say?"

O'Neill had to be humoring her. He couldn't believe her bizarre assertion. She hardly believed it herself.

"He promised to look out for me. And that I would find Deb."

His expression remained dubious. "You've been under a lot of strain."

She took a deep breath in a futile effort to stop trembling. "You're right. Both the voice and apparition were probably nerves."

O'Neill went to a sideboard and returned with a snifter of brandy. A whopping double. Great. If there was anything worse than a crazy woman, she thought, it was a drunk crazy woman.

"Drink this." He handed her the glass and turned to leave.

The last thing she wanted was to be alone. "Where are you going?"

"To get your bed ready. You'll need a good night's rest. We'll leave at first light to hike back to Endless Sky."

He disappeared into the bedroom Deb had occupied. She averted her gaze from the covered window, well aware it was no barrier against a wandering spirit, and stared at the flickering flames. She couldn't allow herself to go to pieces. Not now. Deb was safe for the moment, but her assailant still wandered free, ready to strike again. Trish had to keep her wits about her if she intended to identify and bring to justice the person who had almost killed her sister.

As much as she dreaded being alone, her only alternative was to sleep with O'Neill. And she couldn't let that happen. Despite all her instincts that insisted he was hiding something, she didn't trust herself to resist the longings he stirred in her.

Resigned to a night alone—she hoped she would be alone and not joined by the Cherokee ghost—she chugged the brandy like medicine. Soon, its soporific effect and the heat from the fire had her dozing in her chair. When O'Neill reappeared and gathered her in his arms, she snuggled against him, her inhibitions diminished by emotional exhaustion and a brandy buzz.

Only half-conscious, she didn't protest when he removed her clothes and tucked her between fresh sheets and blankets. She barely registered the brush of his lips against hers and his whispered, "Sleep tight," before darkness claimed her.

SUNLIGHT SLICED THROUGH the tree canopies and glinted on the rapidly melting snow. During the night, the wind had shifted, bringing warm air from the south to disperse the drifts left by the storm. But the trail was still inches deep in snow and Trish's sneakers were soon soaked. The icy misery of her feet increased her pace, making her more anxious than ever to return to the warmth and relative security of Endless Sky.

In the bright light of morning, she flushed with embarrassment at her behavior the previous night. Her Cherokee apparition had clearly been the workings of her overactive imagination and exhaustion. Just like her dreams. She could have sworn she'd heard O'Neill in the kitchen talking on the telephone in the middle of the night. She even remembered looking at the bedside clock at 2 a.m. But at breakfast, O'Neill had laughed when she questioned whom he'd called.

"I slept like a rock straight through the night," he insisted. "You must have been dreaming."

But hearing him in the kitchen hadn't felt like a dream. Of course, the sight of the Cherokee warrior hadn't seemed like a hallucination at the time, either. This morning, rested and secure in the knowledge that Deb was receiving the best of care, Trish hoped her imagination had finished playing tricks on her.

Ahead, O'Neill's sturdy hiking boots broke through the snow, clearing the path. Every now and then, he reached back to give her a boost up the steepest slopes, his grip strong on her wrist. While his actions were considerate and protective, he'd turned aloof and withdrawn this morning, as he'd been the first day she met him, probably regretting breaking his rule about not becoming involved with a guest.

As conflicted as her own feelings were, she could understand his reservations. O'Neill's magnetic appeal was as much a mystery as the man himself. He made her pulse race, her heart pound and sent a burst of excitement, like Fourth of July fireworks, exploding through her when he smiled. She had it bad, but she couldn't understand why. Yes, he was one of the most handsome men she'd ever met, but no more attractive than Coach Brad Larson was in his own way. O'Neill had helped her sister, but most people would have done so under the same circumstances. And he could cook, a trait she found especially appealing in a man. While looks, kindness and culinary skills were terrific attributes, were they enough to engender the strong emotions that consumed her? She didn't think so. Otherwise she'd be gaga over Bobby Flay on the Food Network.

After a long, arduous climb, they finally crested the ridge to the path that led back to the resort. Trish stopped to draw breath. Bent over with her palms flat against her thighs, she stared at her feet to avoid the view that dropped away in every direction. She was certain, if she had the nerve to peek, she could see all the way to South Carolina and Georgia in the morning's clear, crisp air.

She shifted her gaze from the ground to O'Neill. The lines of his face were as sharp and chiseled as the boulders that lined the trail. A strong updraft ruffled his dark hair and he squinted in the blinding sunlight until she couldn't see his eyes. Nor could she read his face, set in its harsh, inscrutable expression. Even in the glare of day, he appeared withdrawn, mysterious, dangerous. The approachable man who had laughed and joked with her at Stevens's hideaway, now replaced by this silent sentinel, seemed as unreal as the spirit of the Cherokee warrior.

Considering her options, she wondered if she should forget the charade they'd planned and report directly to Captain Metcalf when she returned to Endless Sky. O'Neill had already told the sheriff's officer the truth about her identity and the attack on her sister. She'd leave the mess to Metcalf to sort out and discover Deb's attacker. Then she'd check out of the resort and join her sister at the hospital in Asheville.

A sharp crack broke the stillness of the morning air, followed almost instantly by the impact of a projectile against a rock beside her. Before Trish could react or register what had happened, O'Neill launched himself at her, knocked her to the ground and covered her with his body.

The fall forced the air from her lungs. She gasped for breath to question what the hell was happening, but another crack sounded and kicked up dust beside her head.

Someone was shooting at them.

O'Neill wrapped his arms around her and rolled, taking her with him toward the edge of the ridge. A scream rose in her throat. He was forcing her off the ridge, over the mountainside.

She was going to die.

A third shot sounded, but, rolling through the scrubby underbrush and mud created by melted snow, Trish couldn't tell where the bullet landed. She had two alternatives—to scramble back to the ridgetop and be shot, or continue careening down the slope, which seemed to drop off into nowhere. She tried to grab at the nearby bushes to stop her deadly slide, but O'Neill had her arms pinned to her sides. They slithered rapidly downward through mud and wet underbrush on the south side of the slope. Trish held her breath, expecting any moment to launch into thin air for a fatal fall of thousands of feet to the forest far below.

Certain she was going to die, she was flooded with regrets, sorrow at the living that she'd miss, the husband she'd never love, the children she'd never nurture, Deb left with no family—

She came to a jolting halt, still gripped in O'Neill's embrace.

"Close your eyes." His voice was urgent, his ragged breath warm against her ear. "And do what I tell you."

She needed no coercion to follow his advice. Ecstatic not to be flying to her death, she scrunched her eyes shut against the dizzying panorama.

"Just stay still," he whispered. "Let whoever was shooting think we went over the side."

"We did go over the side. And why are you whispering?"

"Sounds carry in the mountains. I don't want anyone to hear us."

"Are you okay? Were you hit?"

"I'm fine. Just stay quiet."

With the muddy, rock-strewn ground at her back and O'Neill's hard warm body covering her, Trish kept her eyes shut and whispered back. "Maybe it's a hunter who's mistaken us for bears."

She felt him shake his head. "We were profiled against the sky. A person would have to be blind to think we were bears. And a blind person couldn't shoot that well."

"But he missed us."

"Probably only because the updraft from

this side of the ridge ruined his shots. But he came close enough."

A tremor shook her. "So those shots were meant for us?"

"Either you or me."

"Or both." She couldn't stop shivering.

O'Neill pulled her closer, encircling her with his warmth. "We'll be okay. But climbing back to the ridgetop will be tough. The terrain's steep."

"What if the shooter's still out there?"

"That's why we have to wait. Make him think we fell to our deaths over the edge."

"What if he comes to check?"

"He's a long way from us," O'Neill said.

"How can you tell?"

"The time lapse between the rifle shot and the bullets' impacts. He's probably on another ridge. He'd need a long hike to reach us, more than enough time for us to make it back to Endless Sky."

"Can I open my eyes?"

"Not yet."

"Why not?"

"We're safe where we are, but the view

will make you dizzy. Just relax and save your strength for the climb."

Relax?

He had to be kidding. They were practically hanging by their fingernails from the top of the world, and he wanted her to relax. She stifled an hysterical giggle. "Got it. Relax, but don't enjoy the view."

With her eyes closed, her other senses kicked it. She recognized the sharp, coppery taste of blood where she'd bitten the inside of her mouth as she fell. The wind keened up the slope, slicing into her skin, accentuating the discomfort of her wet clothes. The damp wool of O'Neill's sweater and his distinctive balsam scent filled her nostrils. He'd pressed his cheek against hers, but whether as protection from the wind or to prevent her from gazing outward, she couldn't tell. His steady heartbeat thudded against her chest, a counterpoint to the rapid rhythm of her pulse.

After lying still long enough for her muscles to stiffen, she breathed a sigh of relief when O'Neill finally shifted his weight and spoke.

"Don't open your eyes. Just do as I say, okay?"

"Okay." He must really think her a wimp, with her vertigo and fear of heights, and he was right. The last thing she wanted was to see how close to the edge they'd come.

"I'm going to stand up now," he said, "but don't move until I tell you to."

She nodded and felt the weight of his body lift from hers. He grabbed her hands. "I'll pull you to your feet. Ready?"

"Okay."

She stood upright, but struggled to balance without her sight. O'Neill released her hands, grasped her shoulders and turned her, staying behind her with his hands steadying her back. The wind at her back indicated she was facing upslope.

"You can open your eyes now," he said, "but don't look down or behind you. Stay focused on the ridge above us."

She opened her eyes, blinked in the morning glare, gazed up the slope and closed her eyes again. How in the name of heaven did O'Neill expect them to climb that steep grade slick with mud? Then again, what choice did they have? Staying where they were until they were hunted down wasn't an option.

"Take it slow," O'Neill said. "Make sure you have both a firm handhold and foothold before you lift your body weight. I'll be right behind in case you slip."

Trish reached above her head, grasped the branches of a large bush and lifted one foot to a slab of stone protruding from the muddy earth. She gingerly hoisted herself a few inches, then continued moving upward.

"That's the way," O'Neill said. "You're doing fine. Keep climbing."

After an agonizingly long time, several slips on the slick ground and pushing her muscles to their limit, Trish reached the top of the ridge. O'Neill scrambled up behind her. Even plastered with mud and debris, he maintained his rugged good looks. She was glad she didn't have a mirror.

Thoughts of her appearance vanished

when she glanced down the mountainside at the trail they'd left in the mud. It ended on a ledge, like the one where Deb had fallen, that dropped off into nowhere. Realizing how close they'd come to dying, Trish felt her already-punished leg muscles threaten to give way.

O'Neill grabbed her arm and pulled her along the path. "We have to get off this ridge, just in case our shooter still has us in his sights."

Trish didn't need to be told twice. The dizzying trail along the ridgetop was preferable to another precipitous descent. She forced her weary legs to hurry.

"I don't get it," she said, her breath coming in brief pants. "Why is somebody shooting at us?"

"Maybe for the same reason Deb was pushed?" O'Neill didn't slow down.

To keep up, Trish was moving at a trot. "But that doesn't make sense. No one knows I'm Deb's sister, except you."

Her stomach clenched at that sickening realization, and the memory of O'Neill on the phone in the middle of the night flashed through her mind. He'd insisted he'd slept through the night, but her recollection was too strong to have been a dream. Had he called in an assailant? But O'Neill as a suspect didn't make sense. He'd done everything to save Deb earlier and to protect Trish from this morning's shooter. Why would he ruin his own plans?

Unless he was covering his tracks, setting up an alibi for later.

She hated where her suspicions led and wondered if her conclusions came from her sixth sense or following too many high-profile court cases in the media.

"Metcalf knows you and Deb are sisters," O'Neill said, "but he wouldn't have told anyone. It would hinder his investigation."

She knew nothing about Metcalf, so she couldn't dispute O'Neill's assertion. "What have we done to make someone try to kill us?"

"None of it makes sense." His long stride ate up the path, bringing them closer to the resort and safety with each step.

"You have to leave Endless Sky. Go to Deb at the hospital. Stay in Asheville under an assumed name, like your sister."

His suggestion had its appeal. And its drawbacks. "Deb and I have to return home to Tampa eventually. If someone wants to harm us, we won't be safe until whoever it is is caught."

Without slowing his steps, he cast her a sideways glance, his demeanor dark and threatening. "I can't make you leave, but I strongly recommend it."

She wanted him to convince her that the secrets he hid had nothing to do with what had happened to her and her sister. But, as much as she was attracted to him, her instincts wouldn't allow her to lay her suspicions to rest. No one had known where they'd been, so how could a shooter have been lying in wait for them this morning unless O'Neill had tipped him off?

"What makes you so sure someone was shooting at me, not you?" Her words came in short puffs, like her breath.

O'Neill, however, wasn't the least bit

winded. He returned his gaze to the trail ahead. "Why would anyone want to kill me?"

"You tell me."

He shook his head. "I'm a nobody. And I have no enemies that I know of."

She wasn't convinced. O'Neill had depths she'd never plumbed. His past, for all his claims of ordinariness, was shrouded in mystery, laden with secrets. Who knew what he was hiding?

"If I'm leaving soon," she said, "we won't need our charade to make people think we're involved with each other."

He shook his head and reached to steady her when she stumbled over a rough patch in the trail. "Hiding your true identity would be smart until we can get you out of here."

She had to laugh, in spite of their dire circumstances. "How are we going to explain our appearance? We look like we've been mud-wrestling."

A ghost of a smile lifted the corners of his mouth. "With any luck, the guests are off on excursions for the day and we can slip in unnoticed."

"What about the staff?"

"To work at Endless Sky, they're required to be discreet. No need to worry about them." His hand still grasped her elbow. "I'll take you into Asheville as soon as you've had a chance to clean up and pack."

The prospect of a long, hot shower quickened her steps. Within fifteen minutes, they were crossing the lawn of Endless Sky, where patches of snow lingered, despite the brilliant sun. The sheriff's command tent still stood on the edge of the drive, but it was empty and the convoy of rescue vehicles had left. The huge log resort, even in the midday glare, appeared abandoned, forlorn and forbidding, its empty windows staring at her like lifeless eyes.

They approached the terrace doors and a tall, middle-aged woman with cropped gray hair and dressed in a smart, navy blue suit stepped out to meet them. "My god, O'Neill, what happened to you?"

"Janine Conover," he said, "meet Erin

Fairchild. Janine's my assistant manager. Erin and I slipped in the mud on the ridge trail." His neutral tone gave nothing away.

"Nice to have you staying with us." Janine's blue eyes flashed a warm welcome. "You probably want to get cleaned up right away. I'll send Ludie May to take your clothes for laundering."

"There won't be time for that," O'Neill said. "Miss Fairchild is checking out after lunch."

"You'll be leaving by helicopter?" Janine asked.

"No!" Trish replied quickly. "I'll go by Hummer."

Janine shook her head. "I'm sorry, but that's not possible."

"Why not?" O'Neill asked.

"Judd Raye used it to transport the guests this morning," Janine said. "Don't you remember? Today's the scheduled hunting trip."

Trish exchanged glances with O'Neill, but his bland expression showed no reaction, and she wondered what thoughts were flitting through his mind. Her own mind filled with suspicions. The outing had been scheduled, so O'Neill had known about it in advance. She recalled again the middle-of-the-night call he'd denied making, the call he'd insisted she had dreamed.

"The guests went hunting?" she asked Janine. "With guns?"

Janine laughed as if Trish had made a joke. "That's how most folks go after bear around here."

O'Neill's eyes darkened and his jaw tensed. The ferocity in his look sent a shiver down Trish's spine.

"Who signed up for this hunting trip?" he asked.

Chapter Eleven

"Let me think." Janine ticked off names on her well-manicured fingers. "Almost everyone. Chad Englewood, Michael Redlin, Austin Werner, Dan Beard and Victoria Westbrook."

Trish flashed another glance at O'Neill, but his eyes were hooded, his expression guarded. Was he thinking, as she was, that everyone on her list of possible suspects had been hunting, with access to a rifle? Any one of the named guests could have fired shots at them on the ridge.

Before she could comment, O'Neill changed the subject. "Any damage from the blizzard?"

Curiosity danced in Janine's eyes. She had to be wondering where O'Neill and Trish had been during the storm, but apparently knew better than to ask. "A few roof shingles ripped away, some trees down near staff housing, but otherwise we came through okay. The guests, however, didn't like being cooped up by the weather. That's probably why so many chose to hunt this morning."

"Thanks for taking care of things," O'Neill said. "I'm sure you're ready for a break."

The assistant manager shook her head. "No problem. I was on my way to the kitchen to approve tonight's menu when I saw you coming. Nice to meet you, Ms. Fairchild."

Janine returned inside and Trish waited until the assistant manager closed the door behind her. "Do you think one of the guests was our shooter?"

O'Neill wrinkled his forehead and frowned. If he'd had anything to do with the shooting, he hid his involvement well. With a smear of mud across his high cheekbone and his thick black hair wild and tousled, he looked more dangerous, more attractive than ever. Except for the anger flashing in his dark eyes, an emotion so intense it frightened her. Was he furious that someone had shot at them? Or angry that the shots had missed her? Her thoughts spun in circles that made her stomach queasy.

"One of them could have taken the shots at us," he admitted. "Too much of a coincidence to think otherwise. But which one, that's the question."

"At least we're safe here until they return." She spoke the words, but she didn't believe them. Her gut was screaming danger. While part of her wanted to throw herself into O'Neill's arms, a more rational segment of her brain urged her to run, to get away from O'Neill and Endless Sky now, to take a terrifying chopper flight out if necessary.

"Get cleaned up," he said quietly, his low voice like a caress. "You have to leave as soon as possible. Even if you have to fly out."

His echo of her intention threw her into more confusion. Stressed and exhausted, she couldn't make an intelligent decision. She needed a shower and some sleep before she could put events into perspective and think straight.

Exhaustion dulled her fears of remaining at the resort. "Unless there's an emergency with Deb and she needs me, I'm not riding in the helicopter. I'll take my chances on waiting for the Hummer."

The lines of his face softened and the anger vanished from his eyes, replaced by a tenderness that squeezed her heart. "Then get some rest. You've had a tough couple of days."

"Will you have someone drive me to Asheville later?" Eagerness to escape the dangers of Endless Sky battled with her reluctance to leave O'Neill. But Deb needed her, and her attraction to O'Neill was irrational, futile at best, dangerous at worst.

"I'll take you," he said, "right after dinner."

"Why wait?"

"When the guests return from their hunting trip, observing them at dinner will give us the opportunity to gauge their reactions. The shooter may give himself away when he realizes we didn't fall to our deaths. Get some rest," O'Neill ordered, "then call me when you're awake."

Isolated and without transportation, what other choice did she have? "Okay."

He turned on his heel and headed toward his residence. Trish, shoes squishing with dampness, entered the hotel. Stepping from brilliant daylight into its dark interior, she waited for her eyes to adjust to the darkness.

An eerie quiet filled the dining room and the light that filtered through the terrace doors didn't reach the corners. Anyone could have been hiding in the shadowy depths, and Trish couldn't see them. A chill shook her, but whether from her wet clothes or the room's spooky atmosphere, she couldn't tell.

A noise sounded behind her, but when she whipped around, no one was there. Muffled voices filtered through the swinging doors that led to the kitchen, but Trish was certain the noise, like the scrape of a chair against the floor, had come from behind, not the kitchen.

With her eyes accustomed to the murk, she hurried through the darkened room to the elevators in the gloomy, empty hall. She couldn't shake the feeling that someone dogged her steps. In the elevator, she pressed her back into a corner, on guard and surveying the empty car until it opened onto her floor.

Feeling foolish at her skittishness, she hurried to her room. She went in and locked the door. Then, remembering that all hotels had master keys, she grabbed a straight chair and shoved its back under the knob so no one could force entry without her hearing. She also checked the locks on the balcony doors, although only Spider-Man could gain access at that height.

After stripping off her wet clothes, she placed a call to the hospital and was connected to a nurse in the recovery room.

"Your sister underwent surgery just

fine," the nurse assured her, "but she hasn't come out of the anesthesia yet."

"When she's awake, will you tell her I called and that I'll be there this evening?"

The nurse agreed.

Trish stepped into the hot shower, soaked the aches from her muscles and washed the mud from her skin and hair. Doubts and questions about O'Neill hammered her, but she had answers for none of them, nothing to clarify her feelings for the man, nothing to either clear or implicate him in the attacks on Deb and herself.

Later, after blow-drying her hair, she fell across the bed, pulled a handmade quilt over herself and dropped into a deep sleep.

And dreamed of O'Neill.

Deep in sleep, she relived every moment of his kiss and reveled in the remembered warmth of his embrace. Her body stirred with longing. She wanted him, more than any man she'd ever met. Her doubts vanished as he made her skin tingle, her heart sing. She found herself back at Quinn Stevens's private hideaway with O'Neill.

Only this time, when O'Neill scooped her into his arms and carried her to the bedroom, he didn't leave. Her every nerve ending hummed with desire and when he laid her on the bed, she pulled him beside her.

He slid his hands beneath her blouse and his touch scorched her skin, setting her afire. She lifted her face to his kiss and opened her mouth to him. Breathing her name like a prayer, he consumed her with a kiss that rocked her to the toes. Frantic with need, she tugged his sweater over his shoulders to expose the hard, smooth muscles of his chest. He pulled away and for an instant, she feared he'd changed his mind, but he quickly shed his clothes. Returning to bed, he undressed her with delicious slowness, trailing his fingers across her supersensitive skin, kissing her neck and breasts until her body screamed for release. Positioning himself above her, he caught her gaze with his deep blue eyes.

"Are you sure?" he asked.

Despite her need, she hesitated.

And her dream shifted. She was no

longer at Stevens's hideaway but standing in the ghostly forest of dead evergreens. The Cherokee warrior with his dark face as ancient as the surrounding mountains faced her. Wisdom and sympathy glimmered in his black eyes.

"O'Neill," the Cherokee said, "he is special to you?"

"Are you asking if I love him?"

"The Cherokee do not have such a word."

"No word for love?"

"We would say that he walks in your soul."

"That's beautiful."

"Then it is true?"

"I don't know. Sometimes he frightens me."

The ancient voice was gentle but probing. "Does he frighten you, or do you fear yourself?"

"How can I be afraid of myself?"

"Do you fear O'Neill will hurt you?"

"What if I let him walk in my soul," Trish mumbled in her sleep, "but he doesn't let me walk in his?"

"You are in great danger."

"From O'Neill?"

"Peril is all around you. Trust no one. But for now, you must sleep."

"I am asleep. This is just a dream."

The ancient warrior's stern features softened with a hint of a smile. "The test is yet to come."

A LOUD KNOCK at the door wakened Trish, and a glance at the clock indicated she'd been asleep for over two hours. Pulling on a robe, she went to the door, unwedged the chair and checked through the peephole. Ludie May, with her weathered face like a dried apple, stood outside with a room service cart.

Trish opened the door a crack.

"The manager sent tea," the maid said.

"O'Neill?"

Ludie May shook her head. "Ms. Conover. Mr. O'Neill must've taken some time off. Ain't seen him for a couple days."

Trish stepped aside and Ludie May rolled in the room service cart.

"Has the hunting party returned?"

"Not yet. You and the Averys are the only ones here."

Trish did a silent tally of the guest list. "Where's Tiffany Slocum?"

"Miz Slocum checked out this morning."

"And Mr. Redlin's companion?"

"She left half an hour ago in the helicopter."

"The helicopter's gone?" Trish didn't know whether to feel relieved or anxious. "Is it coming back?"

Ludie May shrugged. "Don't know."

She removed the cloth that covered the cart to reveal a silver tea service and a plate of cakes and sandwiches. "Anything else you need?"

"No, thank you, Ludie May." The maid turned to leave. "Except to know what to wear to dinner."

"Ain't fancy tonight. Folks'll be tired after huntin'." She left and closed the door behind her.

Ludie May's dialect had turn *tired* to *tarred*, and Trish smiled at the image it conjured—until she remembered that one of those hunters had taken shots at her. She hurried to wedge the chair under the doorknob again before pouring herself a cup of tea and placing another call to the hospital.

DRESSED IN A green-and-russet plaid skirt and a forest-green twin set, Trish took the elevator to the first floor. An uneasy quiet hung in the hallways, and the persistent sense that she wasn't alone raised prickles on the back of her neck. She blamed the unsettling feeling on her strange erotic dream of O'Neill and another ghostly visitation. After dinner, she would put both behind her after O'Neill drove her to Asheville to join Deb. She looked forward to leaving the eerie confines of Endless Sky, and the prospect of saying goodbye to O'Neill filled her with both regret and relief.

Would she stay if her life hadn't been threatened and Deb didn't need her? Probably not. Her attraction to O'Neill was a dead-end street. Although he appeared attractive and compassionate, she knew nothing about what lay beneath his enticing and mysterious facade. She'd longed for passion, but O'Neill, with his closely guarded secrets, frightened her. She tried to assure herself she'd be better off concentrating her hopes for the future on Coach Brad Larson—bland, predictable, and totally nonthreatening—but she couldn't work up much enthusiasm.

Her practical intentions, however, didn't prevent her pulse from speeding when she caught sight of O'Neill in the dining room. He'd changed from his muddy clothes into black wool slacks, a black turtleneck sweater, black blazer and black boots, an unsettling study in darkness. The color accentuated his deep tan and the midnight-blue of his eyes. Glancing up, he met her gaze, and her heart stopped at the heat that flashed between them, even at a distance.

Before she could cross the room to meet him, Chad Englewood shoved back his chair at a nearby table and rushed toward O'Neill.

"Where the hell have you been?" Chad's

angry drunken voice filled the dining room and stopped all conversation. The man thrust his face close to O'Neill's, invading his space.

O'Neill held his ground and cocked an eyebrow. Chad had to be blind not to note the blue flame of anger in his eyes.

"And how is that your business?" O'Neill's low voice, tight with control, carried through the room.

Chad's pale complexion turned purple with rage, a vein bulged in his neck and he punched O'Neill's chest with his index finger. "I came here to find Quinn Stevens. You're the only one who knows where he is, and you'd damn well better tell me."

The slur in Chad's voice and the slight stagger in his bearing indicated he'd overindulged in predinner drinks.

"You should have a seat and cool off, Mr. Englewood," O'Neill said with deadly calm.

"Don't tell me what to do!" Chad was a big man at six-two, but O'Neill was taller. The difference in height didn't deter Chad from grabbing the lapels of O'Neill's blazer. The man might as well have tried to shake a mountain. O'Neill stood immovable, solid as a rock.

"Tell me how to find Stevens," Chad bellowed.

"And lose my job?" O'Neill said quietly. "You're not thinking straight."

Two men rose from Chad's table and flanked him, each with a hand on his arm.

"Chill out, Englewood," the first one warned.

"Kiss off, Werner," Chad growled between clenched teeth. "This isn't your fight."

"It's not O'Neill's, either," the second man said.

"Easy for you to say, Redlin," Chad said. "You've got your millions. Quinn Stevens stole mine, and I intend to get them back."

"Slugging me won't get your money back." With amazing ease, O'Neill pried Chad's fists from his lapels. "But if you'll stop by my office in the morning, I'll give you the name of Mr. Stevens's attorney. Have your lawyer contact him. Let the legal eagles fight it out."

O'Neill's tone, as smooth and deadly as a sheathed knife, stopped Chad cold. The man stepped back, stumbled before regaining his balance and nodded. "Good idea. We'll talk tomorrow. Now I need another drink."

O'Neill flashed a warning to the hovering waiter and Trish guessed that when Chad's drink was served, the alcohol content would be negligible.

Austin Werner and Michael Redlin escorted Chad to his table and O'Neill crossed the room toward Trish.

"Sorry you had to witness that," he said.

"You handled it well."

"Goes with the job. The guest is always right."

"Even when he's drunk and obnoxious?"

"Especially then." His smile lifted the corners of his generous mouth, exposed the white perfection of his teeth and created a dizzy sensation, like dropping too fast in an elevator, in the pit of her stomach. "I've reserved us a table."

He took her arm and led her across the

room to a table for two, tucked into a secluded, candlelit corner.

The intimacy threatened her and she longed for the relative safety of the company of the other guests. She doubted anyone would attack her in front of witnesses, but she didn't trust her feelings for O'Neill. "Isn't this a bit obvious?"

"Part of our cover, remember?" He bent low and spoke softly in her ear as he pulled out her chair.

His breath against her skin threw her heartbeat into a crazy rhythm. "What's the point of a charade? I'm leaving after dinner."

With athletic grace, O'Neill rounded the table and sat across from her. His smile faded and was replaced by an expression she couldn't read. "How's your sister?"

"She's doing great, out of recovery and back in her room." Trish gave him a condensed report of her conversation with Debra.

O'Neill waited for the waiter to serve their salads. "I'm glad she's doing well, because you can't leave tonight."

"Why not?" Trish blurted, so loud that Mrs. Avery, seated at the nearest table, turned and fixed her with a disapproving stare.

"The parkway ranger called an hour after the hunting party returned," O'Neill continued. "Melting snow caused a mudslide across our access road. Not even the Hummer can cross it. And it could take days before it's cleared."

Trish took a deep breath. Maybe flying at night, especially with her eyes closed, wouldn't be as bad as she feared. "Then I'll take the chopper."

"Can't," O'Neill said with a shake of his head.

"Why not?"

"Look out the window."

Trish glanced outside. Ragged flags of mist streamed across the lawn, obscuring the view.

"Visibility's down to zero," O'Neill said. "No one can fly in this weather."

She was in a nightmare and couldn't wake up. Deb needed her, someone at Endless Sky was trying to kill her, a Cherokee ghost haunted her dreams, but she was stuck here. Stuck with O'Neill, who was either the man of her dreams or her worst nightmare. "How long before the clouds lift?"

"Sometimes we're socked in for days." He took a bite of salad, his appetite obviously unaffected by the news. "Depends on how quickly this front moves through and the winds shift."

Her hunger had disappeared completely. She was stranded on an isolated mountaintop with someone who'd tried to kill both her and her sister. She didn't have a clue who that attacker was, but Chad Englewood's outburst had revealed a murderous desperation. He'd had blood in his eye when he'd confronted O'Neill. He sat now, glaring across the room at them as he chugged another drink.

"Do you think Chad could have been our shooter?" she asked.

O'Neill reached across the table and took her hand. His eyes were warm. "Pretend you're enjoying yourself. You look like you're ready to bolt and run."

O'Neill had nailed her intentions exactly. With difficulty, she forced a smile.

"Better," O'Neill said with a searing look that would have melted her bones if they hadn't been frozen with fright. "I spoke with Judd Raye when he brought the group back from hunting. He said most of them stayed together throughout the day. The only ones he lost track of for an extended period were Chad and Victoria. Both had rifles with scopes. Both, according to Judd, are crack shots."

Trish knotted her forehead. "But why would either Chad or Victoria want to shoot you. Or me? It doesn't make sense."

Something flickered in O'Neill's dark eyes, but he merely shook his head. "I agree. Chad is angry because I won't reveal my boss's whereabouts, but that's no reason for murder. And what would Victoria's motive be?"

Jealousy? Trish thought.

Victoria had admitted she was in search of a wealthy husband. But O'Neill, while he had a good job with great benefits, wasn't in Victoria's social or economic league, which ruled out jealousy of Trish as a motive.

"Maybe whoever shot at us wasn't anyone from the hotel," she said. "Same for whoever pushed Deb. Maybe we're looking in the wrong place."

"I filled in Captain Metcalf on this morning's shooting," O'Neill said. "He has his deputies checking the area for strangers and suspicious activities."

"But the wilderness is huge. And the mountains are filled with tourists. What are the chances the deputies will find someone, especially if he's trying to hide?"

"Metcalf's a good man. He'll do his best." O'Neill squeezed her hand. "And I'll get you out of here as soon as possible. I promise."

The waiter removed her untouched salad and served mountain trout, but Trish merely toyed with her food. Throughout the meal, the voice of the Cherokee who had haunted her dreams echoed in her mind.

Peril is all around you. Trust no one.

"Have you ever used a gun?" O'Neill asked.

His question caught her by surprise. "I don't like hunting. I could never kill a living creature."

"I'm talking about a handgun." He tapped the inside pocket of his blazer. "I want you to take this after dinner and keep it with you tonight, just in case."

She shook her head. "I'd be more of a danger to myself than anyone else. Shooting yourself in the foot is a cliché, but there's truth in its origin."

"What if I ask Ludie May to stay with you?"

Trish felt her skin crawl. She'd already felt frightened when she entered the dining room. Now O'Neill was pushing her toward the edge of panic. "Do you really believe someone will try to harm me here, with so many people around?"

"No," he said quickly. "I just thought having a weapon might ease your mind."

She patted her lips with her linen napkin, laid it beside her plate and stood. "Getting out of Endless Sky will give me peace of mind. For now, I'm going to my room. I should call to let Deb know I won't be seeing her tonight."

O'Neill rose from his chair. "I'll come with you."

Trish shook her head. "You should take care of your other guests."

Before O'Neill could protest, she pivoted on her heel and hurried through the dining room. A quick survey revealed that Chad and Victoria had left before her. Trish approached the elevator, but a hand on her arm stopped her.

She whirled around to find Victoria, who'd apparently just stepped from the ladies' room.

"You're a shrewd one," the redhead said with a scowl. "Really cozied up to O'Neill, didn't you? Is he as good in bed as he looks?" Victoria, like Chad, appeared wasted. Her blue eyes glittered and she swayed slightly.

Trish ignored the question. "Did you enjoy your hunting trip?"

Victoria's bright red lips turned down-

ward in a pout. "I had two perfect speci-
mens in my sights, but they both got away."

Suspicions galloped through Trish's
mind. "I heard you were a good shot."

Victoria's expression turned sly. "I am."
She raised her right hand, pointed her
index finger at Trish's head and cocked her
thumb in imitation of a gun. "Next time, I
won't miss."

Victoria's hostility stunned Trish. After
a few drinks, the open, friendly socialite
had turned threatening and obnoxious, and
Trish wanted nothing more to do with her,
at least not until after she'd sobered up.
"Good night, Victoria."

The redhead flexed her thumb as if fir-
ing, then blew imaginary smoke from the
tip of her index finger. "Sleep tight."

Behind Trish, the elevator doors slid open.
Shaken, she stepped inside. Victoria turned
and lurched toward the dining room as the
doors shut. Heart pounding, Trish leaned
against the wall. Tomorrow she was leaving
Endless Sky, even if she had to hike out.

She reached her floor, stepped out of the

elevator into the creepy stillness of the hallway and hurried to her room. Inside, she flipped on the lights and locked the door behind her.

And almost fainted when she turned and viewed her suite.

Drawers had been pulled open and their contents strewn, her luggage upended and its linings ripped. The contents of her purse had been dumped onto the king-size bed.

After checking to make certain the thief was gone, she took only a moment to assess her belongings. Two items were missing: her aunt's diamonds—Trish, distraught over Deb, had forgotten to lock them in the room safe—and her Florida driver's license.

Chapter Twelve

Trish's first instinct was to alert O'Neill. He had been with her the entire time she was out of her room, so he couldn't have been the thief. She'd ask O'Neill to contact Captain Metcalf, even though Metcalf couldn't reach the resort under existing conditions. At least O'Neill had a gun and could keep her safe until the cloud cover lifted or the road was cleared and the authorities arrived.

She rushed from the room and, not waiting for the elevator, dashed down the wide stairs. In the dining room, she found only Redlin and Werner, lingering over their coffee. O'Neill was nowhere in sight.

Trish approaehed a busboy, who was clearing the other tables. "Where's O'Neill?"

The young man wiped his hands on his apron and pointed to the terrace doors. "He left that way. I guess he's gone back to his residence."

"How do I find it?"

"First house on the left, just below the ridge."

Trish bolted through the doors and plunged into the mist. The suffocating fog obscured all landmarks and muffled every sound. For an instant, she lost her bearings and didn't know which way to go.

Fighting down her panic, she stopped, took a deep breath and oriented herself with the lights from the dining room at her back. Operating on memory, she headed where she thought the residences should be. She was in luck; her feet struck a gravel path, and she followed it through the murky mist. Its downward slope indicated she had left the level plateau behind. O'Neill's house had to be close. She moved toward the faint glimmer of light on her left and stumbled against the steps that led to his porch.

With a sob of relief, she climbed the stairs and pounded on the front door.

No one answered, but the door, unlatched, swung open.

Trish hesitated only a moment before going inside. She stood in the dimly lit hallway at the foot of the stairs. "O'Neill? Are you here?"

No one answered, but the sounds from a television drew her up the stairs. Maybe he was in the shower. She followed the noise of the TV to an upstairs doorway and knocked.

Again, no answer.

Gathering her courage, anxious for the security of O'Neill's protection and advice, she turned the knob and went inside. A *CSI* crime drama was playing on the television in a mahogany armoire across from the king-size bed. Light poured through the partially opened door of the adjoining bathroom.

"O'Neill? Are you in there?"

She shut off the television, but heard no response. She was turning to leave when an item on the bathroom counter caught her eye and drew her up short.

Men's hair dye?

Drawn by the incongruous cosmetic, she entered the bathroom. Beside the container of black hair dye on the vanity lay two contact lens cases. Trish flipped open one to reveal dark blue contacts of a depth of hue intended to change eye color. O'Neill was apparently dying his hair black and altering his eyes. Why would a man who hadn't exhibited the slightest hint of vanity want to enhance his appearance?

Unless disguise, not embellishment, was his goal.

Why a disguise, unless he wasn't who he claimed to be?

And if he wasn't O'Neill, who was he?

Where was he?

Trish returned to the bedroom and spotted a desk tucked into a bay window. Although snooping was alien to her nature, for her own protection she needed to know what O'Neill was hiding. She rifled through the top drawer and extracted a passport folder. The photo inside pictured a brownhaired, brown-eyed O'Neill; the name on the passport sent her reeling.

Quinn Stevens.

O'Neill was the Last Man Standing.

Emotions choked her. Disbelief. Disappointment. Betrayal. Fear.

She dropped the passport as if it had burned her, slammed the desk drawer shut and fled the room.

Had Deb come too close to O'Neill's true identity? Was her sister's snooping the motive for the attacks on both of them? And the shots fired this morning—had they been intended for Trish, not O'Neill? But if O'Neill wanted her and Deb dead, why had he rescued them from the blizzard? Her head spun with contradictions. Only one fact came through loud and clear. If he'd lied to Trish about his identity, had anything else he'd said or done been truthful?

She'd wanted to give her heart to O'Neill, but how could she love a man so deeply embedded in lies? For the protection of her heart, if not her life, she had to escape.

In her haste to get away, she stumbled on the stairs and would have fallen if she hadn't grabbed the banister. Righting herself, she watched with horror as the front door swung inward.

O'Neill had returned.

Her legs almost folded in relief when Judd Raye came through the front door. The custodian held a toolbox and glanced up at her in surprise.

"You lost, miss?"

"I was looking for O'Neill." Somehow she managed to keep her voice steady, in spite of her panic.

"He's back at the hotel, talking to the Averys about some kind of problem with their room." The wiry man hefted his toolbox. "I'm here to check the furnace. Anything I can help you with?"

Trust no one, her Cherokee guardian had warned, but now more than ever, Trish needed to escape Endless Sky, to find Metcalf and ask his protection, but she couldn't do it alone. She needed Judd's help.

She settled for telling a partial truth. "My sister's ill and I need to get to Asheville right away. I came to ask O'Neill to help, but—"

"I can take you," Judd offered.

"But the road's blocked." Had O'Neill lied about that, too?

"It is," Judd said, "but I can drive you as far as the slide in the Hummer. It's only a couple of miles from there to the main road."

"But I can't hike all the way to Asheville."

"Won't have to." He pulled a cell phone from the pocket of his overalls. "Soon as we reach the main road, I can get a signal for this. We can call someone to come get you."

"I'll have to change clothes and grab a coat."

"After I get the Hummer, I'll meet you under the portico."

"No, park behind the sheriff's tent, please. I'd rather no one knew I was leaving."

Judd shrugged. "Suit yourself. I'll get the car."

The custodian left, and Trish scrambled down the stairs and out the front door. The fog covered her progress across the lawn and when she entered the dining room, she was relieved to find it empty. Running silently across the carpeted expanse, she took the stairs two at a time to her room.

Minutes later, she again made her way through the fog and across the lawn, this time dressed in jeans, sneakers and a warm sweater and jacket. Her purse, its contents restored, except for her missing license, was tucked under her arm.

The Hummer, lights off, was parked behind the sheriff's command tent with Judd in the driver's seat. Trish opened the passenger door and climbed in.

"Ready?" Judd asked.

Trish nodded. "Let's go."

Afraid Quinn Stevens would appear out of the mist to stop her, she locked her door before fastening her seat belt.

Judd nudged the vehicle forward, its fog lights barely visible in the soupy atmosphere. The Hummer bounced and jolted over the rough terrain, and Trish tried by sheer power of will to hasten their speed.

"You say your sister's ill in Asheville?" Judd asked without taking his eyes off the road.

"Not ill, exactly. She had an accident."

"Thought you was from Florida."

"I am."

"Your sister live up here?"

She glanced at Judd with suspicion, then decided he was just being sociable. "No, she's visiting, too."

"What kind of accident?"

"What?"

"Your sister. What kind of accident did she have?"

She studied the custodian's weathered face, tinged green by the lights from the control panel, but saw only friendly interest. "She fell while hiking and broke her ankle."

He shook his head. "That's a darn shame."

"But she's okay. I had a long talk with her before dinner."

Judd cast her a squinty glance. "If she's okay, what's your hurry to get to Asheville?"

"This place," she answered with a shiver, but kept O'Neill's true identity to herself. "It gives me the creeps."

Judd grinned, revealing a gap from a missing front tooth. "Don't like ghosts?"

"I don't like isolation. I'm used to coming and going as I please."

"Must be nice to be free as a bird. No worries. Lots of money." Longing tinged Judd's voice.

"For now, I'll settle for getting off this mountain."

"After tonight, miss, you won't ever have to see this place again."

She focused on visions of hot Florida sun, balmy skies and white sand beaches, and tried to ignore the chilly gloom that encompassed the Hummer. She didn't know how Judd could find his way through the thick fog but figured he'd made the trip often enough to do it blindfolded.

Her thoughts of home did little to banish the pain in her heart. She'd known O'Neill was mysterious, a man with secrets, but she'd never guessed he was a liar. What other secrets had he hidden from her? She'd been a fool to open her heart to him. He must have thought her naive and stupid, especially when she'd returned his kisses with such passion. In her humiliation and remorse, she had to hold herself back from banging her head against the window in frustration. Quinn Stevens had tricked her, but soon she'd be safe with Deb, with protection from the sheriff's department. Safe from a nameless killer. Safe from her broken heart.

"This is as far as the Hummer goes." Judd interrupted her thoughts. "From here to the parkway, we're on foot."

She gazed through the windshield and swirling mist at a mountain of red clay, boulders, broken trees and rubble, barely visible in the headlights. If not for this mudslide that had blocked the road, she would have left Endless Sky hours ago with O'Neill. Would he have told her he was really Quinn Stevens? Or would they have parted with his deception intact?

She jumped from the vehicle. Rounding the Hummer, she joined Judd, who held a large flashlight in one hand, a backpack in the other.

Trish nodded toward the backpack. "What's that?"

Judd slid the straps of the pack over his arms and settled it between his shoulder blades. "I never go into this wilderness without water, a first-aid kit and emergency supplies."

"Good thinking." She was so rattled, she was lucky to have remembered her purse.

"I'll go first and light the way. You follow close behind."

"Let's hurry, please." The sooner they reached the parkway, the sooner they could use the cell phone. She'd call Metcalf to send a deputy for her.

Judd swung the light in an arc past the edges of the slide, then pointed to a break in the trees. "There's the trail."

He set out in a long-legged stride, and Trish hurried to catch up with him.

O'NEILL WATCHED Janice Conover lead Mrs. Avery toward the elevator. After checking

with the hotel's physician in Brevard, Janice
had given the old woman a sedative to calm
her nerves. The drug had worked quickly,
effectively sedating the woman and halting
her tirade.

But O'Neill had a greater problem than
the lash of Mrs. Avery's tongue. A thief
was robbing the guests of Endless Sky.
During dinner, someone had entered the
Averys' suite and stolen a triple strand of
seawater pearls that had been handed down
through the Avery family for generations.
Forgetful in her old age, the woman had
neglected to lock them in the room safe.
When apprised of the robbery, O'Neill had
remembered Victoria Westbrook's remark
from several days earlier that she couldn't
find her topaz bracelet. He wondered how
many other items had been taken but
whose absence had gone unnoticed.

Janice returned to the dining room. "Mr.
Avery is putting his wife to bed. What an
old darling. I don't see how he stands the
woman."

"She has a right to be upset," O'Neill

said. "I doubt the pearls were insured, and they had tremendous sentimental value."

"We should alert the other guests."

"You call the sheriff's office and report the theft. I'll go door-to-door and remind them to lock any valuables in their room safes."

"One thing's certain," Janice said. "Our thief, whether another guest or a member of the staff, isn't going anywhere in this weather with the road closed."

"True, but there're a thousand places to stash stolen items on this mountaintop."

"I'll call the sheriff." Janice headed for the office.

O'Neill hurried upstairs to check first on Trish. The exquisite diamonds she had worn her first night at the resort made her a prime target for a jewel thief.

She didn't answer his knock at her door, not even when he called her name and identified himself. His instincts on alert, he entered her suite with his master key.

Every light in the room blazed, illuminating the chaos of open drawers, ripped luggage and overturned furniture. Even more startling was the tall and ancient Cherokee warrior, arms crossed over his bare chest, standing sentinel in the center of the room.

TRISH FELT AS IF she'd been walking down the steep, dark forest trail forever. Her knees ached, her calf muscles trembled and her breath came in shallow gasps. "How much farther?"

"Almost there," Judd called over his shoulder.

The man couldn't be human. He wasn't even breathing hard. Trish knocked aside the branches that snapped toward her in his wake and plunged down the rugged slope.

Ahead, Judd's flashlight reflected off a shiny green surface, and he halted.

Confused, Trish stopped alongside him. "That's a pickup truck."

"Yeah. It's mine."

She wouldn't have to call the sheriff.

Judd could drive her into town. "Why didn't you tell me you had a truck?"

"Didn't want to spoil the surprise." Judd turned toward her and the barrel of a handgun shimmered in the beam from the flashlight.

Too late, she realized that in her haste to escape O'Neill and the heartbreak he'd caused, she'd been reckless to rush into the wilderness with someone she didn't know. "Are you working for Quinn Stevens?"

"You mean O'Neill?"

His knowledge of the resident manager's true identity heightened her fears. "What are you going to do with me?"

"What you wanted." She couldn't see his face in the darkness, but his voice was filled with evil. "I'll make sure you never see Endless Sky again."

Even in her terror, her mind connected the pieces of the puzzle. "You're the one who pushed my sister at the overlook."

"Yeah, but not hard enough if she's still alive." His eyes flashed yellow, like a nocturnal animal. "Once I deal with you, I'll have to stop at the hospital in Asheville and finish the job."

Her mind whirred, searching for an escape, a way to save both Deb and herself. "Is Stevens paying you? I'll double it, whatever it is."

"You're just a schoolteacher. Stevens is a billionaire."

"I have a house, a car. They're all yours, if you'll just leave me and my sister alone."

Judd threw back his head and laughed. "And give up a million dollars? I ain't crazy."

Stevens was paying him a million dollars? Trish's knees gave way and she sank onto the trail. Running her hands over the ground, she searched blindly for a rock or branch, anything to use as a weapon.

She jerked when two shots rang out. At first, she thought Judd had fired on her. But she felt no pain and heard only a loud hissing coming from the direction of the pickup truck.

Judd swung the beam of his flashlight in the direction of the shots.

O'Neill stepped out of the trees. The beam of light accentuated the strong angles of his face, the ferocity in his eyes, the vein ticking in his neck. "Drop the gun, Judd."

"Stay where you are, O'Neill, or I'll kill her."

"You shoot her." O'Neill's voice was cold, deadly. "And I'll kill you. You can't run. I've punctured two of your tires. And Metcalf's on the way. You can't escape, Raye. Lay down your gun."

Like a cornered animal, Judd backed toward his truck. "Don't hurt me. I'll tell you everything."

"Like how you stole the jewelry from the guests at Endless Sky?" O'Neill's angry voice cut through the darkness like a sharp blade.

Trish watched in confusion as Judd shrugged off the backpack with his free hand and offered it to O'Neill. "You can have it all back," he said, but his voice held more cunning than sincerity.

Fear must have driven her crazy. If Judd wasn't working for Stevens, why had the custodian attacked Deb? Why had he threatened to kill Trish? Her head spun in bewilderment and her stomach clenched with terror. Judd kept his gun trained in the direction of O'Neill, caught in the beam of Judd's flashlight.

"Throw the pack on the ground and drop your gun," O'Neill ordered.

Judd shook his head. "Got too much to lose. Looks like we got us a Mexican standoff here."

"Why did you push Debra Devlin off the overlook?" O'Neill asked. "Did she catch you stealing?"

"Hah!" Judd hefted the backpack. "These little doodads are just a bonus."

"For what?" Trish said.

"For killing Stevens."

"What have I done to make you want to kill me?" O'Neill said. "I've always treated you with respect and paid you well."

He'd mentioned earlier that Metcalf was on the way, and Trish guessed that O'Neill was stalling for time, waiting for backup.

"You have always treated me right,"

Judd said grudgingly, "but you never offered me a million bucks."

Trish gasped in surprise. "Someone's paying you a million dollars to kill O'Neill?"

Judd's grin, visible in the backlight of his flashlight, was sly and greedy. "You must've really pissed off your former partner, O'Neill."

"Blaine Carter?" O'Neill said in a mixture of surprise and disbelief. "He doesn't have a million dollars. You've been snookered."

"I don't think so." Judd cocked his head.

Trish listened, too, and detected the sound of approaching vehicles ascending the steep grade of the parkway.

"Gotta go," Judd said. "Sorry, O'Neill. This ain't personal."

As Trish watched in horror, Judd switched off his flashlight and fired simultaneously. She flinched at the corresponding barrel flash of O'Neill's gun, and his shot reverberated through the trees. The echo of both shots faded, leaving only silence.

Hunkering down, she cowered in the

darkness, afraid to move or cause a noise that would reveal her position. Although her life was in jeopardy, she feared for O'Neill. She'd misjudged him terribly. He was just a man who'd wanted his privacy. No sound came from his direction. Had Judd shot him, or was he, like her, hiding in the darkness, waiting to assess the situation?

Judd, too, was quiet, but whether dead, wounded or biding his time, she couldn't tell.

She yearned to go to O'Neill, to assure herself he was all right, to thank him for coming after her, but if Judd was conscious and awaiting his chance, any movement or noise that called attention to her position would be fatal.

In the distance, vehicles screeched to a halt, doors slammed, voices sounded, dogs barked. But neither Judd nor O'Neill reacted. Running footsteps thundered up a nearby trail and moments later, a wide search beam swept the area.

The light revealed Judd, lying in a heap by his pickup, his gun and backpack beside him. The beam moved, and Trish followed the light's path.

"On, no!" she cried.

O'Neill, too, lay still where he'd fallen.

Chapter Thirteen

Trish straightened the desks in her classroom, replaced scattered books on the
shelf and watered the pots of pothos and
peace lilies in the windows. Students and
the other teachers had left an hour ago to
begin their Thanksgiving holidays, but she
was in no hurry. Deb was spending the extended weekend with friends in Sarasota.
Trish had refused her sister's pleas to
come with her, so Trish would be cele-
brating alone.

Brad Larson had invited her to have
Thanksgiving dinner with him and his
brother's family, but Trish had declined.
She had finally accepted that, while Brad

would always be a good friend, she'd never be in love with him.

Not as long as she was in love with O'Neill.

With a sigh, she gathered her purse and books and locked the classroom door. Loving O'Neill was an exercise in futility. She'd probably never see him again.

Not that she hadn't tried. After Metcalf and his deputies had arrived that fateful night, an ambulance had whisked O'Neill to the same hospital where Deb had been recuperating. Before O'Neill was out of surgery to repair the wound to his shoulder, however, his staff had formed a perimeter around his hospital room that would have made the Secret Service proud. Two days later, when Deb was fit to travel home, Trish was still trying to visit O'Neill. She'd probably never think of him as Quinn Stevens. All she had gotten was an assurance from the head nurse that he was out of danger and on the mend.

After her return to Tampa, she'd waited, hoping for the phone to ring or a knock on her door, but she'd heard nothing from O'Neill. Not even a hint on the news or in the papers of what had happened, although Deb had certainly tried her best to gather the details of the story. Without proof and specifics, her editor wouldn't go to press with the exposé about the confrontation between Stevens and Judd Raye.

Trish's belongings, complete with her aunt's diamonds, neatly packed with a handwritten note from Janine Conover, had been shipped to her Tampa home, and she'd finally given up on hearing from O'Neill. The man was a recluse, she kept reminding herself. He didn't need or want anyone else in his life.

If only she could feel the same way. No matter how hard she tried, she couldn't drum O'Neill from her thoughts or her heart. Crossing the parking lot to her car, she breathed in the chilly air swept in by the morning's cold front. Its crispness reminded her of the mountains and O'Neill's hideaway, and longing threatened to overwhelm her.

Driving along the Suncoast Parkway, she considered continuing north instead of taking the exit to her house. Endless Sky was only twelve hours away by car. But when she imagined the chilly reception she'd receive, if O'Neill was still there and hadn't left for St. Thomas, she turned toward home.

Her house was her sanctuary and usually brought her joy and comfort, but this afternoon, she prowled the empty rooms like a caged animal, beset by questions, racked with yearning. She decided to call Brad and accept his invitation for tomorrow after all, if for no other reason than to avoid her current misery and to keep from going stir-crazy.

Her doorbell rang before she reached the telephone. Peering out the front window, she spotted a dark sedan by the curb.

Déjà vu. Had the FBI returned?

Peering out the peephole of the front door, she glimpsed only a pair of broad male shoulders and the back of a brown-haired man's head. When she opened the door, the man turned to face her.

"O'Neill!"

His expression was solemn, his eyes wary. "Hello, Trish. May I come in?"

Stunned, she stepped aside for him to enter. He looked different. Not only were his eyes and hair brown, instead of midnight-blue and black, but fine lines of fatigue etched the corners of his eyes and mouth, and a hint of pallor lightened his usual tan.

She followed him into the living room and sat across from him. "Are you all right?"

He nodded. "I will be, after a few more weeks of rest."

He looked bone-tired.

"Shouldn't you be resting now?"

He shook his head. "I would have been here sooner, but I had to get at the truth first." His gaze burrowed into hers.

"Telling the truth," she murmured, remembering his deception and trying to resist his pull on her. "Must be a new experience."

"Not everything was lies."

"Just minor things, like your name."

"O'Neill is my name. It's my middle name, my mother's maiden name."

"And you're not really the manager of Endless Sky."

"Yes, I am, several months out of the year. The job gives me a chance to meet people and interact with them without the mythical Last Man Standing getting in the way."

"I thought you liked your solitude."

"Sometimes. But mostly I enjoy being with people who like me for myself and not my money." He leaned forward and clasped his hands between his knees. "How's Deb?"

"Mending. She's in a walking cast for several more weeks."

"I'd like to see her. Give her the interview and photos she wanted."

Trish blinked in surprise. "You're kidding?"

He shook his head. "It's the least I can do, after what she went through because of me."

For weeks, the sisters had plied Captain

Metcalf's office with questions about the motive for the attack on O'Neill, but "ongoing investigation" had been the only response. "Do you know why Judd pushed her?"

O'Neill nodded. "Maybe I'd better start at the beginning."

"Take your time." *Stay forever.* She couldn't believe O'Neill had sought her out and was sitting in her living room.

"Blaine Carter told the authorities the entire story, after they traced his phone records and documented his payments to Judd Raye." He shook his head, his eyes sad. "I'm sorry I killed Raye. I only meant to wound him to keep him from hurting you, but it was literally a shot in the dark."

"So this whole plot was driven by Carter's wanting revenge?"

O'Neill leaned against the back of his sofa and closed his eyes for a moment. "More greed than revenge."

He looked so weary, she wanted to go to him and hold him, but she wasn't sure yet where she stood. "I don't understand. What did Carter stand to gain from your death?"

"Ten million dollars," he said with a grimace. "When we were partners, we took out key man insurance policies on each other. When I sold my shares of the company to Carter, I let my policy on him lapse. Unknown to me, Carter kept the life insurance on me."

"Why did Carter wait till now to try to collect?" Trish asked.

"He needed someone else to do his dirty work. Maybe it took this long for him to line up a killer."

"And if Judd had killed you, Carter would have paid him a tenth of the face value of the policy?" She shivered at the extent of both men's greed.

"That was the plan."

"But how did Deb fit in?"

"Judd feared she'd overheard him on the trail, on his cell phone with Carter, telling him how he intended to kill me. He couldn't take the chance that she'd reveal their plans."

"And the shots at us on the ridge?"

"Judd fired them at me, not you. He slipped away from his hunting party long enough to get off a few rounds when he spotted us on the ridge. A crime of opportunity."

"But he was going to kill me, too. You heard him."

"Judd was too greedy. The million Carter promised him wasn't enough. Judd stole almost another million in jewelry from the guests. And when the police went through the backpack that held the jewels, they found your driver's license."

"That's how he knew I'm Deb's sister."

"According to Carter, Judd feared Deb might have told you about the phone call she'd overheard."

Trish shook her head. "The irony is that Deb heard nothing."

"Now Judd is dead and Carter's going to prison for a long, long time." He leaned forward again and winced.

"Your shoulder, it's okay?"

"Eventually. The doctors assure me there's no permanent damage."

"That night I left with Judd, how did you know where I'd gone? And how did you reach us so fast?"

"After Mrs. Avery reported her pearls had been stolen, I went to your room to make sure you'd locked your diamonds in the safe."

"But I'd already left with Judd."

He nodded. "Your Cherokee friend told me."

"You saw the ghost?"

"He didn't look like a ghost. At the time, he seemed as real as you do now. To catch up with the Hummer, I borrowed Henry's all-terrain vehicle."

She cocked her head and studied him. "Why come after me yourself? Why didn't you just alert Metcalf and let him handle it?"

"Because, in the words of our Cherokee friend, you walk in my soul, Trish. I couldn't let anything happen to you."

Her heart leaped at his words, but she remained cautious, fearing she'd misunderstood. "Do you know what it means, to walk in your soul?"

He stood, grasped her hands, and pulled her to her feet. "It means I love you, Trish. I want to spend the rest of my life with you."

She closed her eyes, afraid if she opened them, she'd find she'd been dreaming and O'Neill would be gone. But her eyelids flew open when his lips claimed hers. She threw her arms around his neck and arched on tiptoe to kiss him back.

A moment later, while she caught her breath, he grasped her shoulders and gazed deep into her eyes. "What we shared at Endless Sky wasn't a lie."

"But you barely know me."

"I know what's important. Alicia taught me to be wary around women. I've known too many who are more enamored of my money than me. But from the first time I met you, I realized you're different. Honest, unpretentious. And you're satisfied with yourself and your life, a life dedicated to others." A boyish grin lifted the corners of his mouth. "Doesn't hurt that you're gorgeous, too."

"I don't know what to say."

His grin disappeared. "God, I'm an idiot. I thought you felt the same way."

"I do." She lifted her hands to his face and caressed the strong planes of his jaw. "I'm just…surprised. I tried to see you after the shooting, but your staff wouldn't let me. And then when I didn't hear from you—"

He covered her hands with his. "I couldn't come until Metcalf had completed his investigation and answered all the questions. I didn't want to place you or your sister in more danger."

She smiled and her vision blurred with tears of happiness. "The ghost was right, O'Neill. You do walk in my soul. I've been miserable these past few weeks without you."

"Let me make it up to you."

"How?"

"Spend Thanksgiving in St. Thomas with me."

"St. Thomas?"

"My parents are at Endless Sea and I want you to meet them. And I especially want them to meet you."

"You're sure?"

He wrapped her in his arms and spoke against her hair. "I've never been more sure of anything in my life."

Epilogue

Last Man Standing Wed in Private Ceremony

TAMPA—Billionaire and eccentric Quinn Stevens married Patricia Devlin, a Tampa native and teacher, in a private ceremony attended by family and close friends at St. John's Cathedral last month. In an unprecedented public appearance, Stevens and his bride posed for pictures on the church steps.

Stevens's wedding marks the second time in six months that his name has headlined the news. Last December, in a startling exposé by *Tribune* reporter Debra Devlin, now Stevens's sister-in-law, Stevens recounted the attempt on his life by his former partner, Blaine Carter, who has since been indicted for conspiracy to commit murder and is now awaiting trial.

Reliable sources disclose that Stevens, one of the wealthiest men in the nation, did not sign a prenuptial agreement. When asked why he refused the usual legal safeguard, Stevens replied, "Everything I have is my wife's, because she walks in my soul."

The couple is honeymooning at an undisclosed location.

* * * * *

*Don't miss the debut of
Charlotte Douglas's upcoming title,
PELICAN BAY,
a Maggie Skerritt mystery,
in Harlequin Next,
coming in September 2005!*

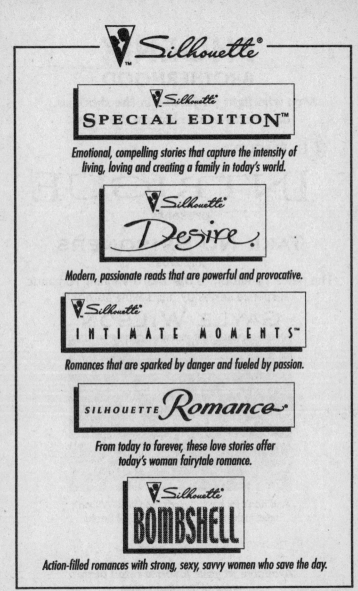

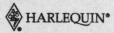

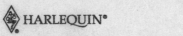